PRAISE
FR

MW01505148

"Following Ami into the small port town of Wolf-sound feels like coming home, even if 'home' doesn't usually come with a robust supernatural community, a magical bookstore, an unsolved murder, and, perhaps worst of all, Lucien and his infuriatingly irresistible smirk. The Ink that Bleeds was witty, charming, and undeniably cozy."

— CHRISTINA BOEKELOO

"hdkkakdjjsjdfsa"

— DAN WELLS

"This is a lay-back-in-the-recliner-near-the-fire-place book if I've ever read one. Curious, quaint, and comfortably surprising, it goes for your throat like a corgi—which is to say, it nuzzles and wants head pats."

— COOPER D BARHAM

THE INK THAT BLEEDS

PIPER J. DRAKE

Piper J Drake

APOLLYCON 2023

ALSO BY PIPER J. DRAKE

London Shifters series

Bite Me, Sing for the Dead, Survive to Dawn

Triton Experiment series

Hunting Kat, Tracking Kat, Fighting Kat

True Heroes series

Extreme Honor, Ultimate Courage, Absolute Trust

Total Bravery, Fierce Justice, Forever Strong

Stand alone titles...

Siren's Calling

Red's Wolf

Finding His Mark

Gaming Grace

Evie's Gift

Keeping Cadence

Want the earliest updates, sneak peeks, and exclusive content
from Piper? Sign up for her newsletter.

For Corbin, our very own fuzzy butt.

ONE

P lease don't let anyone be dead.

Ami climbed out of the car and gazed up at the weathered storefront, still the same after decades. Her heart warmed at the sight. "Here it is. The Mystic Bookstore in Wolfsound."

The bookstore was an actual brick-and-mortar, two-story building on a neatly maintained lot flanked on either side by a wooden privacy fence more than a little taller than her. Of course, she was five foot nothing, so a lot of things towered over her. She was taller than she had been the last time she'd been here, though, and she could see past the tempting stacks of books in the front windows to the bookcases inside. Even though the interior was dark, it felt as though the storefront windows were looking back at her.

There should have been a shadow in there—the silhouette of a kind woman whose face Ami couldn't remember. Who had let Ami read any book she wanted, as long as Ami was careful with it.

"You weren't kidding, the place actually exists. It needs a presence on the internet." Helen pulled a carry-on-sized bag out of the trunk, reached back into the car, then grunted. "You're going to have to get your massive duffel bag."

"Yup." Ami tore her gaze from the bookstore and turned to retrieve her large bag. Between the carry-on and the duffel, she had enough clothes and toiletries to spend a month figuring out what was going on with the bookstore. Maybe her life too.

That might be asking too much.

"So I'll need to catch a ride back to the ferry before dinner." Helen pulled out her smartphone, probably to set herself a reminder in case she lost track of time.

"If you miss the ferry, you could always stay the night here with me," Ami offered. It'd make the first night in a new place a little less intimidating if she had her best friend with her. "We could camp out in the book stacks and read all night."

Helen laughed, her black curls bouncing around her round face. "Oh no. I've got work first thing tomorrow and I will not be able to wake up in time to make the whole journey back to the mainland and down to Seattle in time. Besides, I do not do tiny towns. I came here to make sure this place actually exists and that you have a reasonable place to stay, then I will be just a text message away."

It was already a huge favor that Helen had come all the way out to the San Juan Islands with Ami. They both used to be based on the East Coast, out of the Philadelphia area. Helen still was and she had arranged her schedule to work out of her company's Seattle office this month just to be within panic distance if this journey of Ami's turned out to be a bad idea.

Actually, Ami was sure it was a terrible idea. She just had a soft spot for terrible ideas.

Helen sighed and stepped closer to Ami. "We've got most of the day before I need to head back. That's plenty of time to get you settled, or decide to call it quits and go back to Seattle together."

True. Ami pulled an envelope out of the sleek backpack she used in lieu of a purse.

"Is that a wax seal?" Helen leaned in to take a closer look. "You told me about this, but we only talked about what it said, not how it looks like a wedding invitation."

Both the envelope and sheet of paper within were made of heavyweight paper, cream-colored and elegant in their lack of design or patterning. There was only an embossed design: a stylized tree surrounded by words.

The Mystic Bookstore
Wolfsound, WA

The wax seal was a deep red, the color of blood when it first wells up from a vein, before oxygen has a chance to brighten its color. Ami shook her head. Morose thought to have while she was standing in the light of midmorning.

"Definitely not the happy tidings that are supposed to come with a wedding invite," she murmured. The letter had held bad news only barely softened by a hopeful promise.

Ami would have done without the hope if it had meant the bad news wasn't true.

"Yeah." Helen's tone had turned wry, and she shuddered. "Maybe we're reading into the wording too much. Maybe 'gone' means something happy, like 'won the lottery and left.'"

Helen walked up to the front door and tried to pull it open. Then she jiggled the doorknob. The door remained closed, despite the sign in the window saying it was open. "Huh."

3

"Bookstore's closed, dears!" a voice called out from across the street.

Ami turned and found the speaker sitting under the shade of one of those large umbrellas set in the center of a round glass tabletop set in a wrought iron frame. Three chairs were gathered around the table, all currently occupied. One of the occupants, the woman, waved, then beckoned. Ami glanced at Helen over her shoulder and shrugged, then made her way across the street.

"Should we grab your bags?" Helen asked.

Ami shook her head. "We can see them. They're not likely to go anywhere."

She gestured up and down what was technically the main street of the sleepy harbor town. Just a block from the waterfront, the buildings here were an eclectic mix of some very old, a lot of recently restored, and a smattering of new buildings. None of them were over three stories tall and they all looked as if they went together, giving the town the feel of a very old coin polished to a shine. Few people were out and about in the middle of the morning on a weekday.

"Good point." Helen quickened her stride to catch up with Ami.

The two of them approached the table, and the woman smiled up at them. She could have been sixty or she could have been eighty, it was hard to tell. Her skin was pale and smooth with just a hint of a blush over her cheeks and forehead, like the petals of a tea rose. The corners of her eyes crinkled as she smiled, and her thin lips were stained berry pink. Her grey hair held streaks of brown and she wore it long, in a loose braid down her back. A riot of escaped wispy strands framed her face.

Her blue eyes were bright and her gaze was sharp as she took in Ami and Helen. "It's a bit early for tourist season.

I'm afraid you've got bad timing if you're visiting. The bookstore won't be open for a while."

A memory tugged at Ami's mind, but she couldn't quite access it. "We have all day."

One of the other people at the table shook his head. He was a bit younger, maybe. He was Asian with an oval face. His hair was short and spiky on top, mostly black but fading to a generous salt-and-pepper at the temples and through his neatly trimmed beard. His makeup was subtle, mostly in neutral shades, enhancing his contour and giving him a flawless complexion. Honestly, Ami wished she could do as good a job with her makeup on a daily basis. Mostly, she saved the effort for special occasions.

"Bookstore won't be open today." He tipped his head to one side. "Probably not tomorrow either."

Ami finally looked at the third person in their casual party: Southeast Asian, hair shaved close to his skull, his skin dark and weathered as if he'd been exposed to the sun and sea all his life. The feeling of familiarity tugged harder at her. Dark eyes watched her, waiting. Impulse took hold, and she lifted her hands in front of her chest, then pressed her palms together so that each of her fingers was touching its counterpart. She bowed her head slightly so the tip of her index fingers just barely touched her nose, bending her knees as she did. "Sawasdee ka."

"Sawasdee ja," the third man responded in kind. "You've been away a long time, Amihan."

The other two sat straighter in their chairs and started studying Ami. The woman cackled. "Well, I don't know how you recognized her all grown up, Det, but here she is. Maybe the bookstore will open soon after all."

"Wait, wait, wait." Helen held up her hands and looked from the three of them to Ami. "So, if you remember her from when she lived here way back when she was a little kid, then you've been here a while and you can tell us if this letter is for real."

Ami's stomach jumped up and twisted inside her. If anyone would know, they would. She remembered now.

"Please, tell me no one died to leave me this place," she whispered. "Maybe they retired or moved away?"

She placed the letter on the glass table between the three of them. They all leaned in and read the letter, though it was the woman who picked it up and held it back out to Ami. "I'm sorry to say it's true, dear. You're the new owner of the bookstore."

"So the previous owner did die then." Helen placed a comforting hand on Ami's shoulder.

"Oh yes." The woman looked up at them both, nodding. "She was murdered."

LUCIEN ALLARD SCOWLED as he stalked toward the main street of town. One or two retirees out watering plants or tending their lawns glanced his way and waved but didn't try to stop him for a chat. Maybe it was his purposeful stride and no-nonsense expression. More likely it was because he'd only just moved back to the island and he'd been gone long enough for the locals to still feel he was an outsider—especially the humans.

It was just as well. He didn't have time for this anyway, but he also wasn't going to run down his . . . guest in broad daylight either.

He paused and took a deep, slow breath, noting the scents in the air and sifting through the information they gave him. Taffy might have a solid head start, but he didn't need to have his target in his line of sight to follow the little jerk.

He was faster, stronger than Taffy, and had opposable thumbs in at least two of his forms. He should be more than a match for one questionable witness. Yet here he was.

It wasn't like it was that hard to guess where Taffy was going anyway. He'd be less irritated by the little guy if said witness wasn't also far too stubborn for his diminutive stature to back up.

Voices carried toward him as he turned onto the main street of town, just a couple of blocks down from the bookstore. Laughter and expressions of admiration. Of course. Taffy was popular. He made friends instantaneously—basically the opposite of Lucien.

"Oh, aren't you adorable!" a distinctly feminine voice exclaimed.

Sure. Most people reacted that way to Taffy. Lucien was the only person on the island who wanted to toss Taffy into lockup and maybe tie him up to keep him where he was supposed to be and not running loose in the streets of town.

Not that there was that much traffic at this time of day during this time of year. Tourist season would have been a different matter. Still, it was hard to protect a witness who was determined to constantly return to a potential crime scene. The fact that Lucien was responsible for said protection was also a sore spot because Lucien was not what represented law enforcement in this town. At least, not human law.

"Hello." A different voice, equally as feminine. Even at a distance, this one did things to him. "Are you supposed to be out here all alone? No leash?"

There was a darker timbre to that voice that teased his

ears, and he wanted to hear more. Besides, rather than just being charmed by Taffy, the speaker was obviously possessed of a practical mind. He lengthened his stride and saw Taffy, not at the bookstore like he'd anticipated, but across the street at the witch's apothecary.

Lucien also took in the number of people around Taffy: two standing and three sitting. The three town gossips were in their usual morning location, which was no surprise. Some things didn't change, even over decades, especially when it came to long-lived supernaturals. Normally, Lucien would have avoided them at all costs. It wasn't that he didn't like the three of them. It was just that he didn't enjoy having his business all over town faster than the speed of social media. And each of them had a knack for digging up any bit of information a person wanted to hide.

He didn't let any of that break his current forward pace, but damn, he was not looking forward to this. Instead, he focused on the two people currently showering Taffy with affection. The cheeky corgi was jumping up on his hind legs, resting his front paws on the rather shapely thigh of one woman. As she crouched down, the little bastard actually tried to crawl into her lap.

"Oh, that's just Taffy. He's a local," Bridget said. The human witch waved a hand gracefully in the direction of the corgi while leaning back in her seat at the table with the other two town gossips. "He's such a good boy, there's really no need for a leash."

"Still." The woman looked up from her crouch, holding the wriggling corgi in her arms as he did his best to lick her jaw. "With no owner in sight, a dog really shouldn't be loose and off leash. Even if he has perfect recall, there's no one to recall him if he gets into something dangerous. A leash can be as much for the dog's safety as for anyone else."

She wasn't wrong, though there were plenty of people who might argue with her.

It was Det who saw Lucien first, the old trickster's gaze locking on with an impact Lucien could feel even from this distance more than a block away. A corner of Det's mouth lifted in a smirk. "Here comes the person responsible for Taffy now."

Oh no, the old serpent had not just thrown Lucien under the bus that way.

The woman straightened, keeping Taffy cradled in her arms as she stood. The corgi had stopped squirming, at least, apparently content to remain in her embrace and pant. She was from out of town and so was the person at her side, presumably the one who had exclaimed earlier and now muttered, "Hello, Naughty Dog Owner. Did you bring a leash? You don't have to put it on the dog. I promise."

"Helen," the other woman whispered, sounding scandalized.

He smirked. Couldn't help it. He did have a sense of humor, contrary to what most of the town might believe.

The breeze carried her scent to him. Everything inside Lucien sharpened and told him to pay attention. Light notes of plumeria flowers tickled his nose with their almost fruity fragrance, then the deeper aroma of ylang ylang took over his olfactory senses with its earthy richness.

Helen must be the one who had asked if he'd brought a leash. She smelled of sugared violets and tart plums. Both of the women were human.

He settled his gaze on the woman carrying Taffy. Her brown eyes were the shade of burnt umber, and only her widening pupils gave him any kind of sign that she was less than confident about his proximity. She had the situational awareness to sense the danger he represented even if she probably didn't know he could be anything but human, and he liked that.

She also didn't show any signs that she might make some fake excuse and scamper off to remove herself from an uncomfortable situation. He liked her even more for it. Helen remained to one side, a steadfast friend, but didn't step up to meet him head-on.

No. It was Taffy's new best friend who held her ground despite the big bad wolf approaching.

"Luc, these nice folks just arrived," Bridget said brightly. She brushed a few brown and silver strands off her forehead, the movement attracting his attention for a split second. It was enough to break the building tension between him and the newcomer holding Taffy. "You remember Ami, don't you? She and her family lived here on the island for a while. You two might've gone to school together. Ami, do you remember Luc?"

He shifted his gaze back to her and stared. She stared back, her mouth forming a slight O.

His mind hit him with several ideas for what he might want to do with her mouth, and he ruthlessly stuffed those thoughts into a mental box and locked it. Those were inappropriate with an audience, though he wasn't averse to mulling them over later.

"It's been a long time." Ami spoke slowly, never looking away. Her cheeks flushed a very attractive dusky rose.

Ami. He tasted the name inside his head, unwilling to say it out loud. It didn't quite seem to fit. Amihan—his memory supplied her full name to him. Yeah. He liked that better.

He gave her a slow nod. "Welcome back to the island, Amihan."

"Everyone calls me Ami."

"I like your full given name better."

She narrowed her eyes. "Fine, Lucien."

He liked the sound of his name coming from her even more.

Silence fell, awkward. No one seemed willing to break it, and he wasn't willing to let go of the eye contact they had going. It'd been a long time since he'd experienced any kind of chemistry like what was happening between him and Amihan now. He hadn't even touched her yet.

He hoped she would let him touch her.

Taffy barked, short and sharp, then turned his head to bury his nose in Amihan's hair.

Amihan gave in and laughed, tilting her head to give Taffy a snuggle. Lucky dog. Her eyes sparkled as she smiled at Lucien. "So did you need your dog back?"

"Not my dog." That came out more brusquely than he'd intended. Also, not very helpfully. He tried again. "Taffy's the bookstore corgi. I was taking care of him, because they don't really have the means to take care of him over at the police station."

"Oh." Amihan's eyes dimmed a little. Sadness? Maybe. "He lost his person."

Lucien didn't answer. He didn't know what he could say. It was the truth.

"He found you, dear," Bridget said. "And you're the new owner of the bookstore. Maybe you're the answer to a few of the questions floating around here right now."

"Wait. What?" Lucien focused his attention on Bridget.

Jin spoke up. "You all go catch up. It's coming up on lunchtime and Det has to open his restaurant. I need to go open up my salon. Bridget has the apothecary to open or Mr. Delaney won't be able to stock up on his regular order for enlargement cream."

That was a completely unnecessary piece of information, and Lucien wanted to immediately forget it. Bridget smiled serenely.

"Let's just get you situated," he said to Amihan. Anything to get away from the town gossips and maybe get his day back to some kind of semblance of what he'd had planned. "Where are you staying while you're in town?"

"At the bookstore," she answered promptly. She shifted Taffy's weight so she could free up one arm and snagged a paper from the table. She waved it at him. "That was the plan, anyway."

"Well"—he glanced over at the bags sitting in front of the bookstore that must have been hers—"both our plans for today may have just gotten a little bit more complicated."

CHAPTER

TWO

"Maybe the door was just stuck." Ami stood in the now-open doorway to the bookstore, examining the doorframe. "Wood tends to swell and warp in high humidity places."

She stepped inside and carefully set Taffy down. The corgi ran ahead of her a few steps, then turned and dropped his jaw in a happy grin. He didn't seem inclined to run anywhere or go checking on the status of his home. Actually, she had the distinct impression he was waiting for her.

"No. I swear the doorknob was locked and was not turning," Helen insisted from behind her. "Whatever. It opened for you. That's what matters. Keep going, I've got the carry-on and we can let Mister Naughty Dog Owner get your massive duffel bag."

"Not actually the dog's owner." The dry reply came from over Helen's shoulder.

Ami hurriedly moved to one side to make way for Helen before peering around the doorjamb. Lucien Allard really did have her bag in hand.

The man was tall. Well, a lot of people were taller than

her. He had to be almost a foot taller than her, though. Rangy and lean, with hints of a very nice physique under his collared polo shirt and fitted jeans. He was one of those fair-skinned people with cool undertones who probably burned in just a few minutes in full sunlight. It was good for him that this was the Pacific Northwest, which tended to have a lot of overcast, even stormy, weather. A few strands of platinum blond hair fell across his brow in a way she thought only happened in photoshoots or movies.

Helen made a face and rolled her eyes at Ami, then mouthed the words *Oh Emm Geee so hot!*

Ami glared at her, rethinking whether the title of best friend still applied.

Once Lucien entered, he strode past Helen and Taffy, heading past the cozy sitting area and the main book stacks to the little doorway at the back. He was long-limbed and moved with confidence. The rear view was also very, very nice.

She shut her eyes. No ogling people. Not a good idea. Nope.

His voice, deep enough to send shivers through her, floated back to where she was standing. "Stairs up to the private living area are back here. I'll take this up and leave it at the landing so you can choose what room you want to stay in."

That was thoughtful. Yes. She'd focus on the considerate actions and not what the sight and sound of him were doing to her. No need to get carried away, even if her underwear was in the bag he actually was carrying. Ami opened her eyes before she could start fantasizing and then stared after him, at a loss for words. It'd been about two decades since she'd last interacted with him—otherwise, she knew nothing about him. It was amazing she even remembered his full given name.

Then again, he'd remembered hers.

"So"—Helen gave her a shit-eating grin—"things are looking exponentially more promising, in my opinion. I'll just run across the street and check out that apothecary. It's got a whole display of bath-and-body products in the front window and I might want to buy some to take home with me. I'll just leave you to settle in and . . . reacquaint yourself."

"Hel—" Too late. Her friend had bolted out the door and left her.

Taffy was standing just inside the doorway at the back, probably so he could keep track of both the person upstairs and her at the same time. He looked at Ami with his head tilted at a quizzical angle.

Ami considered her options. It didn't make sense to go after Helen. Following Lucien up the stairs might make sense. She did need to figure out where she'd be staying, and while it didn't seem that anyone was even questioning the idea of her staying here in the bookstore, a letter did not make for any kind of official transfer of ownership. There had to be someone responsible for the paperwork when it came to this business and property, and she had hoped to meet with them to figure out the particulars of how she was supposed to take over the bookstore.

If she decided to take over the bookstore. That was still in question.

She turned in a slow circle. She couldn't remember ever thinking about this place over the years, but she was comfortable standing here now. There were two big windows at the front, with sills deep enough to allow for tempting book displays or holiday decorations. There was a small counter near the front, situated to allow whoever was behind the register a clear path to either the front entrance or the back doorway, and an open stairway down to the basement level. The bookcases were full of books from end to end, with more titles turned on their sides and placed in the spaces left between the books on their shelf and the shelf above. Despite how overstuffed the shelves were, they still gave a reasonably neat impression.

"I checked your furnace and fuse box. Seems like everything is working okay." Lucien returned from upstairs. He slowed as he approached her.

Taffy trotted to her and sat on her left foot. She wasn't exactly sure where she was going to go yet, so she let the corgi stay there.

"Just like that?" she asked quietly. "It's okay if I stay here?"

Lucien studied her for a long moment, catching her gaze again with grey eyes the color of storm clouds. It was an intense experience, having his full attention. He had a way of completely focusing on her when he spoke to her that was just shy of unnerving.

Finally, he shrugged. "I admit, a lot of us in town tend to take any suggestions from Bridget, Jin, and Det as a matter of course. I have questions about how you're supposed to take over here, but there's no reason why you can't stay upstairs while we're all figuring that out."

Taffy barked and flopped on his side, then did a little wiggle on the floor.

Lucien dragged his fingers through his platinum blond hair, which was just long enough on top to be attractively disheveled but shorter and clean-trimmed around the sides. "It'd be good if there was someone to watch after Taffy too."

She let her mouth drop open as shock jolted her. "You're doing this because you don't want to take care of a dog?" She stiffened with indignation. Taffy's person had died—the owner of this very bookstore. Someone Ami felt she'd known as a child, and no, she couldn't remember the woman, but Ami was certain she had been kind.

"What?" Lucien lifted an eyebrow at her.

She huffed. "Maybe you don't intend to come across that way, but I'm wondering why you're so ready to foist off the responsibility of caring for Taffy onto some stranger from out of town."

"Because I've got a lot of other responsibilities to attend to," Lucien shot back. "And you're not a stranger, even if it has been a long enough time that I don't know a whole lot about you. But Taffy obviously likes you and that furry butt is actually a good judge of character. So why not let him stay with you and let me get back to my work? Do you not want to have a little company?"

She was staring at him with her mouth open again. His gaze dropped a fraction and he smirked slightly. She shut her mouth and winced as she did it, hard enough to click her teeth. "This is just very confusing. Who sent me the letter telling me I'd inherited this bookstore? Is there anyone who can tell me what is expected? Next steps? Maybe a solicitor or a lawyer or somebody? There has to be paperwork or something to officially take over the bookstore. I can't imagine I just move in."

"I can't help you much there." Lucien shrugged. "I don't know about any letter. I can give you the number to the police station. You probably want to connect with them anyway. The police chief is the one conducting the investigation into the death of the bookstore owner."

Irritation pricked at her skin and she scowled at him. "Thanks for your help."

He grinned. "No problem."

Heat built up, and she was sure her face was flushed. He had to know she had intended to be sarcastic. She pressed her lips together and breathed in slowly through her nostrils. Then she stuffed all that irritation and frustration deep down inside. He was eager to leave and go on about his day. Fair. He was not a person who could be of help. Noted.

No reason to hang on to anyone who didn't want to be around her. She'd made that mistake enough in the past. She could manage on her own.

"Fine. Go ahead and leave Taffy." She gave him her most polite smile. "Have a good rest of your day."

He stilled, maybe a little surprised at her abrupt change in attitude. If he had been hoping to get her to beg for help, he was both sorely mistaken and a jerk. She would not be giving him the satisfaction of being a damsel in distress. She just kept her smile plastered in place.

Let him sit in the awkward silence.

"I'll come by later and drop off his food and dog bed." Lucien sounded uncertain.

She didn't change her smile at all. "Okay."

"Okay then." It might have been her imagination, but she thought the muscles in his rather angular jaw tightened.

Another silence, then he strode out of the bookstore without another word. The door closed right on his heels with a light slam.

Huh, she hadn't seen him touch the door. Maybe there had been a gust of wind.

THAT DOOR HAD LITERALLY HIT him in the ass on the way out.

Lucien turned to glare but there was no way Amihan could have crossed the distance from where she stood to shut the door on him so quickly. No human could have. Plus, there was no one visible through the glass panels set in the door. Not even Taffy. The door must have closed on its own.

Weird.

He shook his head. There were so many other things he needed to get back to. So why was he still hung up on how that woman had completely shut down on him in there? It was as if she'd taken all the sparks and energy he'd been admiring and shut them away. And the cold in her voice had been something else.

He had the distinct impression something had happened between the space of one breath to the next, like she'd revised whatever her first impression of him had been. He'd definitely smelled her arousal when he'd walked past her into the bookstore earlier.It was why he'd taken her bag upstairs in the first place, because he'd enjoyed being admired by her. But then he'd riled her up and she'd completely dismissed him.

What, just because he hadn't played to her obvious call for help, he was suddenly dropped in the useless category? Well, he didn't need to waste any time on anyone like that.

It wasn't as if either of them had real reasons to hold on to their childhoods anyway. She hadn't seemed to remember. And if he wasn't worth remembering to her, he could finally let go of the memories stuck in his mind like irritating burs caught in his fur.

He shook his head a second time, resisting the urge to

indulge in a full-body shake. There was no good reason for him to continue standing in front of the bookstore either. He put one foot in front of the other and headed toward home.

"Luc!"

Lucien stifled a growl. He hadn't gotten more than a handful of steps away and already, someone was pouncing on him.

"What's this about a new bookstore owner?" Sheriff Mel Altesse came striding toward him. "Did you just come out of there? Where's Taffy?"

Mel walked right up to him until they were almost toe to toe, not something anyone else in the world would dare do. It would have been extremely ill-advised if Mel hadn't been Lucien's best friend, and even then Lucien wouldn't have allowed it if Mel had been a supernatural. Mel was human—one of the very few humans aware of the supernaturals integrated into this small island community.

"Taffy is inside." He decided not to bother answering the first two questions because thinking about the woman inside the bookstore churned up his emotions. Now—pop! There she was, inside his head again, with her dark eyes and rich scent.

"As the sheriff, I should have been notified when a witness has been moved to a new location," Mel said, their tone severe. "You were entrusted with his care. Now, he's with some stranger? And this person has access to a potential crime scene unsupervised?"

Knowing about who was a supernatural in and around town wasn't a requirement for the town sheriff, but it certainly made dealing with the random, inexplicable occurrences that came with close proximity to supernaturals somewhat manageable. After all, the humans as a whole weren't aware that the myths, legends, and night-mares actually lived among them.

A nurturing community like Wolfsound was hard to come by. It made the oldest and most powerful of the local supernaturals inclined to invest a certain amount of effort into maintaining the delicate balance required to preserve the mixed community. But this was still a small town, and as unfortunate as it was, overzealousness wasn't going to help find the killer faster.

Frustration and the urge to hunt both surged inside him, but he locked them down. Too many young wolves let their energy overwhelm their patience and spooked their prey prematurely. Lucien wanted the murderer found and brought to some kind of justice every bit as much as the rest of the town. But he was a patient hunter. Mel needed to be too.

"Taffy is a Pembroke Welsh corgi. It's a stretch to call him a witness, especially since we don't actually know for sure that he was with Nancy when she died." Lucien kept his voice low, trying to slow Mel's momentum. "She also didn't die here, so is this really a crime scene?"

Mel was as tall as Lucien was, only a touch leaner, and not quite as broad as him through the shoulders, with slight curves that they chose not to bind. They had similarly fair skin and sharp facial features and the same way of lifting their chin when they were feeling particularly stubborn. He and Mel could have been siblings, honestly, with their closeness in height, build, and mannerisms. But Mel's hair was that shade of brown just light enough to be mistaken for blond in summer, and their eyes were hazel.

And they were human. It always came back to that, and he could never forget it, because he'd forgotten to keep this difference in mind once as a child and someone had been hurt as a result. He wouldn't make the same mistake again.

He stared at Mel until they dropped their gaze and swallowed hard. Mel wasn't afraid of him, and he valued that in their friendship, but it was important to their survival that they always kept their wits about them when dealing with any supernaturals. They couldn't get carried away, no matter how justified they were either as a person or as a representative of human law.

"I need to meet this person and ask them a few questions." Mel lifted their gaze back to meet his. Their tone was even and calm, indicating that their mind had caught up with the rush of momentum they'd built up hurrying over here.

He nodded. "I'd suggest a trade. The lady inside has a lot of her own questions. Have fun with that."

"Ow!" The muffled exclamation came from inside the bookstore, followed by sharp barking from Taffy.

Mel moved toward the door, and he turned to follow close on their heels.

Amihan stood behind the counter at the register, holding her hand and grumbling under her breath. "I touched one thing, one, and find the biggest splinter in existence. I could stake a vampire with this thing."

Lucien snorted. He was absolutely certain Sebastian would have loved that. Probably for the best that it'd be hours yet before the mayor rose with the setting sun and came to investigate the new presence in town.

"Everything all right here?" Mel's voice had dropped almost an entire octave, bringing Lucien's attention back to the people in the room.

Taffy had reared up on his hind legs and rested his front

paws gently on Amihan's thigh again, ears forward in concern.

Amihan looked faintly embarrassed, dusky rose staining her cheeks again. "Oh, yes. Sorry about that, officer. I was just starting to explore and got snagged on a splinter under the counter here."

A twinge of concern stabbed him in the chest, and he ruthlessly buried it. It was just a splinter, damn it. Still, he stepped around Mel and the counter to take a closer look. "There's probably a first aid kit around here. If not, Bridget will have one across the street."

"It's not a big deal." Amihan looked up at him with wide eyes, then her eyes narrowed. "I thought you left."

"You were loud." He turned to go find the damned first aid kit, then paused mid-motion. "Did you touch anything in this drawer?"

"Hmm? No." Amihan shook her head. "I was going to put my letter in there because there's already a few documents in there. Seemed like a good spot."

"Documents?" Mel came around the counter and stood close enough to brush shoulders with Amihan. "I searched here the other day and there wasn't anything here. I'm Sheriff Altesse by the way, you can call me Mel."

Mel flashed a charming smile at Amihan, and Amihan seemed to blush even harder. "Amihan Chanthara. You can call me Ami."

Lucien gritted his teeth and went to go find the first aid kit. Seriously, Mel had just been about to come stomping in here full of officious police attitude. Now they were practically oozing charm all over Amihan like the woman was the most attractive game in town.

He was not about to admit that she was.

There was a first aid kit on a tiny shelf just through the

doorway opposite the stairs. He couldn't remember if he'd noticed it earlier, but hell, it had been a day for memory playing tricks on him. He grabbed it and returned to the two behind the counter.

Mel had the letter out on the counter next to a document that must have been in the drawer. Lucien set the first aid kit down and opened it, then took out a pair of latex gloves and wrestled them on before ripping open an alcohol wipe. He held out his hand and raised an eyebrow at Amihan.

She let out a huff. "It's just a splinter."

He shrugged. He wasn't about to tell her he was doing it as a basic precaution. Even if it took a lot more than a few intermingling drops of blood, cross contamination from a werewolf could force her body to mount an immune defense, and he didn't want to be responsible for giving her a fever.

Despite her words, she placed her hand in his. Just that contact sparked the chemistry between them. He tamped it down as he examined her tiny wound. There really was a sizeable splinter embedded in the pad of her middle finger. Another pang hit him. It probably did sting.

"Better not to let little hurts become more serious infections," he murmured as he swiped the area, the cotton wipe snagging on the tip of the splinter.

At least it looked like it would be easy to get out. He discarded the alcohol wipe and reached for the tweezers. As he carefully got hold of the end of the splinter, Amihan took a breath and let it out slowly, her hand relaxing more in his grasp. Good.

The splinter came out with one even pull. Blood welled up on Amihan's fingertip and he had to fight the urge to close his mouth over it, let the taste of her blood spread over his tongue.

Mel cleared their throat and grabbed Amihan's wrist, pulling her hand out of his. The move caused a droplet of blood to fall and splatter the document on the counter. Lucien read the words in bold at the top:

Last Will and Testament of Nancy Greene

How had Mel missed that when they'd searched?

Amihan pulled her hand back, free of both him and Mel. "Oh, I'm sorry."

"Not your fault," he said gruffly.

"Not at all," Mel agreed.

Mel moved to brush the blood away, but it had soaked into the paper immediately. "Well, I'll have to make a note as to how that happened. I'll be taking these in to the station with me as evidence."

"Why?" Amihan asked. She stuck her fingertip in her own mouth and sucked lightly.

Lucien suppressed a groan. It only got worse as the scent of Mel's arousal hit him too. He and his best friend were both attracted to the newest lady in town. Classic.

Mel cleared their throat. "Nancy's will could represent motive and we have a few suspects to investigate. This could help to clear them or give us additional insight into the case. I'll take the letter you received too."

"One second, then." Amihan pulled her phone from the back pocket of her jeans and took pictures of both her letter and the will. "I at least want record that these are what I saw before you took them."

Smart.

Mel must have thought so too because their grin only widened. "If you find anything else, or need anything at all, you can call me anytime. Let me put my number into your phone."

Amihan handed over her phone.

While Mel was distracted, Lucien picked up a small Band-Aid and waved it at Amihan. When she would have taken it from him, he jerked it back and held out his other hand. Amihan's blush spread across the bridge of her nose and over the delicate shell of her ears, but she placed her hand in his. He unwrapped the Band-Aid and placed it securely over her fingertip for her.

"Thank you." Her voice made parts of him tighten especially low in his abdomen.

"No problem," he murmured, removing the latex gloves. It was quick work to clean up the mess from his minor first-aid ministrations.

"So, Luc, I think you were headed out. I've still got a few questions for Amihan and you said she had some questions for me." Mel's voice might have been louder than it needed to be with all three of them crowded behind the counter.

"I don't want to keep you from all the other responsibilities you have to attend to," Amihan said, looking him straight in the eye.

He felt like he'd been slapped. Sure, that's what he'd said. He did have plenty of other things to be doing. Plus, he'd just decided he wasn't going to stick around for an irritation like her to hook into his fur and cling. But he'd been helping, and she seemed to appreciate it. Now he was being dismissed. Again.

He scowled. "Maybe try to be considerate of our sheriff's time too."

His temper rode him as he left. What was it about this woman that got under his skin?

THREE

A mi woke with the sun warm and cozier than she had imagined she could be in a new place. Taffy groaned next to her, and she realized he must have joined her in the guest room sometime during the night. All of the previous owner's personal effects were still spread throughout the upper floor of the building, and Ami hadn't felt comfortable taking over the primary bedroom.

Lucien had dropped by again last night, after Mel and Helen had left, and dropped off Taffy's bed and food bowls.

Ugh. The man was infuriating, with his arching eyebrow and stupid smirk. He was also too freaking attractive for words, and he had a knack for getting her so flustered and angry, she flubbed whatever point she was trying to make, mid-argument. She couldn't even remember what they'd been arguing about. Heat flooded her face even as she thought back to it.

After Lucien had left, it had been quiet, and the bookstore seemed too big a space to explore. The previous bookstore owner had been murdered and no one seemed concerned about Ami sleeping there. It was unnerving, but she also felt that it was too late to disturb someone to get a room at one of the bed-and-breakfasts in town. Besides, Taffy would have let her know if anything dangerous came into the building.

She'd gone around and made sure all the doors and windows were locked, then went upstairs to make the guest room her space to start. She wanted just one small nest of blankets and pillows and warmth she could think of as hers before she began to introduce herself to the rest of the building.

The corgi's company was probably why she'd managed to get toasty warm. He was cuddled up to her side. It was comforting, really, to know there was someone else in the building with her. It hadn't taken as long as she'd thought it might to fall asleep.

As she sat up, Taffy got up too and then shook himself all over. Then he dropped low over his forepaws, his fluffy butt in the air, as he stretched his long back.

"Ooh. Good stretch." She ruffled his ears, and he gave her a doggie grin.

Stretching wasn't a bad idea. She lifted her arms above her head to stretch her own muscles and get some circulation going.

Since this entire venture was a fresh start for her, maybe spending a couple of minutes every morning stretching was a good thing to incorporate into her new routine. While she was at it, she was going to leave her phone on the nightstand and not check her email or social media. She didn't want to start her days that way anymore. She'd check all of that once she had breakfast in front of her.

One of the ways she wanted to begin this new phase in her life was by intentionally starting her days off with habits that made her feel good—mentally, physically, and emotionally. She deserved to prepare herself to face the day, not tumble into the day as soon as she was conscious, trying to catch up with any situations that happened somewhere else in the world while she caught a few hours of sleep for herself.

An hour later, she'd taken care of morning personal necessities. She dug a notebook and her favorite fountain pen out of her carry-on. Taffy ran ahead of her down the stairs and barked at the back door.

She opened the back door and found it led out onto a nice flagstone patio with a small patch of green lawn. The modest yard was enclosed by the wood privacy fence she'd noticed from the front of the bookstore, and garden beds lined the perimeter of the fence with a variety of early flowers already emerging—mostly daffodils and tulips. One small cherry tree was raining delicate white petals across the area as a breeze swept past. She didn't remember the backyard, but then, she had very few memories from her childhood years on the island.

It was one of the reasons that man got on her nerves so easily. There was something so familiar about him, compelling. But she didn't know him, and she was supposed to be working on building this whole new life for herself, step-by-step. Her thoughts kept wandering to Lucien, and she didn't need that kind of distraction. At least, not right away.

Taffy returned from doing his business in the back corner of the garden, near what seemed to be a compost bin. Well, she'd figure out the logistics of caring for this yard along the way. There were probably other, more urgent tasks in need of her attention.

She turned and headed back into the bookstore, then sat on the barstool behind the counter and opened up her notebook. It was time to get her thoughts organized and make a few lists. She tapped the back end of her fountain pen against her lips before she set the tip to the page.

She'd need a list for groceries. Someone had at least cleaned out the refrigerator, and there hadn't been much of anything in the pantry. Maybe Nancy hadn't enjoyed cooking. She'd also need to figure out next steps for taking over the bookstore. There was also getting acquainted with her neighbors and learning the layout of the town.

After another minute, she ran upstairs and came back with a stack of sticky notes. She decided the chalkboard on the wall behind the counter would work for the time being, and she set up column headers: Triage, On Deck, In Progress, In Progress (on hold), and Done. Then she let her brain pop up whatever task came to mind. She neatly jotted down a task on a sticky note and placed it under Triage. She placed one or two urgent ones under On Deck.

She had an entire cloud of sticky notes developing under Triage when she heard a knock on the front door of the bookstore. Taffy sprang up from where he'd been laying with his head in his paws, watching her. He led the way to the door as she looked out.

There was a man standing there, obviously waiting, but standing back a polite distance from the door. He was of average height and medium build, with brown-black skin and short hair trimmed close to his scalp. The corners of his eyes crinkled when he smiled and he gave her a wave through the glass.

She found herself smiling in return, but then hesitated as a pang of nervousness twinged in her chest. The previous bookstore owner had been murdered recently. Was it really a good idea to just answer the door? But then again, it was morning, and it was a small town. People were bound to be curious, and she'd just put a sticky up on her board about making an effort to get acquainted with her neighbors. She wanted to become a part of this community.

Lucien had said Taffy was a good judge of character. She took a deep breath and opened the door, prepared to slam it shut if her new corgi friend gave the slightest sign of rejecting their visitor.

"Hi," he said in a quiet tenor. "I'm Trey. Trey Stevens. You're the new bookstore owner?"

"For the time being, yeah." Ami wasn't sure it was a certainty just yet, though Mel had seemed to accept it yesterday. If the sheriff wasn't concerned, Ami probably shouldn't be, but there were probably still legal hoops to jump through to get ownership officially transferred to her name. "I'm Ami."

"Nice to meet you." He didn't make a move to come inside, and Ami realized she was standing in the doorway.

"Come in." She backed up and held the door for him. "I'm not ready to start selling books again, so I'm not sure I can be of help."

"Completely understandable." Trey stepped inside and leaned against a bookcase. "I only wanted to come and offer help, if you needed any. I'm sort of a regular, so I might be able to answer questions you might have about the day-to-day of the bookstore, or the town. Whatever."

He had a pleasant voice with a gentle cadence. While he was studying her with interest, it felt more like the candid attention Bridget or Det or Jin had shown when she'd arrived yesterday. It was nothing like the intensity Lucien had or the overt attraction Mel displayed. While Ami had felt complimented, it had been a whole lot for day one, and she hadn't really had time to process it yet.

"That's really nice of you." She turned to pick up her

notebook and pen, then flipped the page to some of the questions she'd jotted down that Mel hadn't been able to answer. "Actually, I do have some questions you might be able to help with, if you don't mind."

"That's a nice fountain pen." Trey's eyes had lit up. "Doesn't that one have a vacuum filling system too?"

"Hmm?" She smiled brightly. "Yes! I got it as a gift to myself last year after finishing a major project. It's super easy to refill and it holds significantly more ink than any of my other fountain pens. It's my go-to for travel or if I think I'll be writing with it all day."

He grinned. "Nice. I've got a few fountain pens myself, but haven't gone for one like that yet. Most recently, I went for this slim design from Japan because it was a limited production and I didn't want regrets if it becomes too hard to get a hold of."

They launched into a discussion of fountain pens that even Helen would have bailed out of after a few minutes. Before Ami knew it, she'd retrieved her modest travel case of precious fountain pens and her stash of inks so they could head out to a nearby eatery and test inks on a few sheets of paper she always brought in her carry-on for exactly that purpose.

Trey grinned. "This is great. What kind of lunch do you usually like? I'm happy to give you some suggestions about the options in town."

Ami gathered up her pens, checking to make sure all her inks were properly sealed. "That was on deck to do today."

She gestured vaguely to the chalkboard behind her.

"I saw that." Trey nodded while studying the sticky notes. "Is this the start of a kanban board?"

Happiness washed through her. He was a kindred spirit for sure, a new friend, hopefully. It was still wise to move them someplace a little more public to get to know each other better, but so far Trey just seemed to be a curious person looking for a new friend too. She was hopeful for that.

She moved to the board, stepping over Taffy, who was sleeping stretched out on his back with his legs splayed out, and tapped a sticky note. "Yeah. Explore food options is on deck for today, along with acquiring some basic groceries. I like to cook most of the time."

Trey opened his mouth to say something but was interrupted by another knock at the front door.

"Oh!" Ami headed to the door. "I probably should leave it unlocked, but I'm really not open yet."

"Neighbors will be stopping by to say hello," Trey said, remaining by the counter. "There were posts on all the town social media platforms. It's how I knew about you."

"Seriously?" Ami asked. Then she got a good look at who was at her door and considered not opening it.

Lucien Allard stood there. He might have had an idea of what she was thinking, or maybe he'd heard her last comment, because he was giving her that look of his again, like he was daring her to do something. She wasn't sure what. Just something.

Lucien waited, amused, as emotions seemed to run across Amihan's face. She stood on the other side of the door, presumably deciding whether she should open it. He'd heard Trey's voice inside, and the other werewolf's scent lingered on the landing outside the front door of the bookstore. Lucien was here more for Trey's safety than to seek out Amihan again.

33

That was his story and he was sticking to it.

Still, it was extremely entertaining to rile up Miss Amihan Chanthara, and if he was here anyway, why not mess with her? He lifted an arm above his head, leaned against his forearm in the doorway, and smirked at her through the glass.

There was that spark in her umber eyes he liked and the slight narrowing of those same eyes before she pressed those sweet lips together. She reached out and opened the door—

—only to have it snap back in his face.

He blinked and straightened. That had come close to actually hitting him. Through the glass, he could see the surprise in her wide eyes too. She hadn't done it on purpose. They both looked up and examined the doorframe from their respective sides of the door. After a moment, she reached for the door again, more carefully, and opened it.

"Are you okay?" Her voice held actual concern.

She definitely hadn't done it on purpose. He cleared his throat, having forgotten whatever clever thing he'd been planning to say. Instead, he answered her honestly. "Yes, just surprised."

"Us too." Amihan took a step back, implicitly inviting him into the bookstore.

Taffy stood, watching him, ears up and twitching with their usual inquisitiveness. The other werewolf had remained back by the counter, solemnly waiting for whatever Lucien had to say.

"Maybe I'll take a look at the spring in the door-closing mechanism later this evening." Lucien glanced up at the door from the inside. "Wouldn't want it to close on you or future customers and cause an injury."

"You don't have to do that." Amihan held up her hands

palms out, waving them a little. The words had spilled out very quickly. "I can find out who to call for household repairs. I'm sure I'll have a list of things to address by the end of the week anyway."

"It's probably an easy fix. No trouble. I'd rather address it myself than risk my physical well-being every time I find myself in your doorway." He studied his nails but watched her out of the corner of his eye, enjoying the way her face flushed at the implication.

"Why are you here, by the way?" Her voice had gone cool again.

Uh oh, better back off a little. He didn't want her to shut down again. "Not here for the pleasure of your warm and welcoming personality, unfortunately. It's in Trey's best interest that he not visit the bookstore and its new owner alone, at least for the foreseeable future."

Trey's shoulders hunched. Good. The other werewolf should have known better. This was an unnecessary risk, and for what? The bookstore wasn't even officially open yet. He didn't smell any arousal between the two of them, which would have been a surprise in any case. Trey was ace. Not unheard of among werewolves, but also not something that would ever be a secret. Sexuality was reasonably obvious to werewolves because scent and pheromones carried so much information.

Regardless, coming to the bookstore and spending any kind of time alone with the new bookstore owner was an invitation for negative scrutiny. Completely unnecessary. Lucien didn't like for any of his fellow pack members to put themselves at risk, much less for no good reason.

"I came to find out why Trey came to visit, when he's a person of interest in the investigation related to the recent change in ownership of this place." Lucien answered her but kept his gaze on Trey. "People could come to some unfortunate conclusions."

Trey kept his gaze on the floor andseemed to shrink further in on himself. But he offered no defense of his actions, no explanations.

Frustration built, awakening a slow burn inside Lucien's chest. Lucien hadn't taken over leadership of the pack yet, but he was next in line. He'd been gone for a few years, studying in the UK among humans at a university and connecting with other packs overseas. He'd returned to bring fresh perspective back home.

He held a deep love for the pack and every one of its members. It was his duty to protect them, but he couldn't do that if they put themselves in harm's way. While he could assert his authority in person, the members were taking their time to place their trust in his standing orders when he wasn't directly there to enforce them.

Amihan stepped forward, breaking Lucien's line of sight on Trey. Taffy joined her, standing by her left foot.

Lucien shifted his gaze to meet the defiance in Amihan's. He lifted an eyebrow in question. He couldn't risk saying anything to her without voicing his anger too. She didn't know what it meant to intervene between a senior pack member and another werewolf. Her action was a challenge nevertheless, and he would not let it go unaddressed.

"Trey is a welcome guest in The Mystic Bookstore," she said, quietly. Her voice trembled slightly, but considering the way her feet were planted shoulder-width apart and her hands were balled into fists, her anger was superseding any possible fear. She was definitely prepared to fight over this.

Admiration came grudgingly, and his anger abated.

"You've made new friends quickly."

He didn't clarify whether he was talking to Amihan or Trey. Behind her, Trey had lifted his head, his golden-brown eyes wide with surprise and a more vulnerable emotion. Well, her defense of him had surprised Lucien too.

"This is my bookstore. It's important to me to make this a safe space for my guests." Amihan lifted her chin, still stiff and defensive. "And Trey has been great company. He's very knowledgeable about fountain pens."

Lucien lifted both eyebrows this time. That was quite the statement regarding her territory and how she intended to protect it. He didn't know much about the bookstore, but he did know the bookstore owner's intent would have an impact on the core nature of the place. It wasn't just a building.

He glanced past them both to the leather-bound traveler's journal on the counter, stuffed full of inserts, and the fountain pens tucked into a case. Ah. There was the shared passion. He rubbed his jaw to cover his amusement.

"Fine." He almost chuckled at her startled expression. She hadn't been expecting him to back off, he guessed. "Let's be clear, Amihan, I'm here as a friend to Trey. This small town is like any other, which means not everyone is going to like everyone else. There's a few people who would love to go running to Mel spinning a tale they cannot ignore, insisting they take a suspect into custody for public safety. I'm here so busybodies can't say Trey is harassing the new bookstore owner."

"Oh." Her stance relaxed.

Next to her, Taffy sat. Not that there was much of a change, since the distance between the corgi's rump and the ground was only a couple of inches. But Taffy's jaw dropped open in a relaxed doggie grin.

A low rumble broke the heavy silence in the room. Lucien, Trey, and Taffy all looked at Amihan. She stepped back, away from all three of them. "Excuse me! I had a light breakfast."

Trey's mouth stretched into a smile. "Exploring food options was on deck, according to your kanban board."

Kanban board? Lucien studied the sticky notes on the chalkboard more closely. Ah. So it was. Apparently she liked to visualize her work. The embodiment of the overachiever, made more dangerous because she seemed to be extremely organized and efficient. She'd already identified a lot to be done in just a morning to begin getting a handle on things here. It would be good to get her out to rest her eyes and take a break. Trey too.

And it was definitely Trey Lucien was taking care of— his pack member. That was his responsibility here. Pack business.

"Why don't I take you both out to lunch. You two can continue whatever discussion you have going about paper and pens and ink, and I can glare at judgy townsfolk."

"I thought you had a lot of work to do," Amihan said hesitantly.

He shrugged. "My friends come first, and I support friends making new friends. Besides, glaring at people is on deck for me today."

Again, he didn't specify whether he planned to glare at her or other people. Trey coughed into his fist, obviously covering a laugh.

The corners of Amihan's mouth tweaked upward. She nibbled on a corner of her lower lip. "Let me run upstairs and get my wallet."

He'd said he would buy them lunch, but he refrained from calling after her. Maybe she liked having her wallet on her whenever she left her home. She was a person of color, and there were places out there where it was absolutely necessary to have multiple forms of identification. Not because it was the law, but because people were unfortunately not all good at being humans—even the humans.

He would make certain Wolfsound was never that kind of place for her, or anyone else. It was a part of the reason he'd gone out into the human world for his higher education before coming home.

As she came back down the stairs, Taffy hopped up and danced around her feet. The three of them headed toward the door just as another shadow stepped onto the landing in front of the bookstore. They all paused, and Lucien fell back to stand next to Trey as Amihan moved to open the door before the visitor had to knock.

Before Amihan could say a greeting, a petite Asian woman with a sleek bob gave a sharp nod of her head and held up a thick document envelope. "Amihan Chanthara, new owner of the bookstore, I am Matsumoto Rio and I have a business proposal for you."

Amihan didn't take the package. She also didn't step back to invite the woman into the bookstore.

Lucien thought this was ridiculous timing. But then again, the town gossips had announced Amihan's presence all over social media. Still, he didn't like the energy Miss Matsumoto was projecting toward Amihan. Her body was screaming intimidation and power play.

Lucien moved to stand at Amihan's shoulder. "Before we go past introductions, perhaps it would be good to know that Miss Matsumoto is also a person of interest in the case of your recently deceased predecessor, specifically because of that business proposal."

CHAPTER

FOUR

"Taffy!" Ami stumbled on the path in the darkness.

Ahead of her, Taffy paused and looked back, giving what sounded like an encouraging woof. She didn't need encouragement, though. She needed him to come home with her. She was starting to feel sympathy for Lucien and what must have been his predicament the day he'd first encountered her on the island. Had it only been yesterday?

In the space of one day, she'd met a dozen or more new neighbors or townsfolk, all curious about what her plans might be for the bookstore. That wasn't even taking into consideration the business proposal waiting for her, still in its envelope after Miss Matsumoto had dropped it off. She had left after Lucien dropped his bit of helpful trivia.

He'd been rude. Ami had been too startled to think of anything to say. Matsumoto Rio had gone too quickly to even try.

A whole lot had been happening between yesterday and today, and she'd kept Helen up-to-date with frequent texts.

It helped Ami process what was going on. But as soon as she'd told her best friend about lunch with Lucien and Trey, Helen had lost any semblance of control and started texting suggestion after ridiculous suggestion of what she could do with the handsome platinum blond who was definitely no longer responsible for Taffy's well-being.

Speaking of which, internally, Ami was now said responsible person, and Taffy was still headed out on his own adventure through walking trails in the woods. Granted, this was an island. He wasn't going far. She was also reasonably certain there were no bears or cougars in the San Juan Islands. But she'd thought she heard a wolf howl last evening, or maybe a coyote call. She wasn't super familiar with either one. If even a large stray dog was loose in the night, she was not willing to take the chance with Taffy. The corgi was big of heart and not so tall in stature. He was not going to win a fight with any of those possibilities.

"Taffy." She pitched her voice with a little more bite to it, and the dog stopped again and rolled such that he was doing a wiggle in the grass on the side of the dirt path. "Cute, but let's be done now. Come."

He rolled to his feet but didn't move toward her. She shouldn't go toward him, she knew she shouldn't. He'd think he didn't have to listen to her, or maybe he'd mistake this for a game of tag. They stood there looking at each other for a minute, then Taffy took off at a trot again.

"Damn it. Taffy, no." She walked after him, trying to keep him in sight. The sun had set a half hour ago, and darkness fell fast in the forests of the Pacific Northwest. The moon was past half full, enough to provide some light, but she still wished she'd thought to bring a flashlight.

She'd been out like this in the past. There was a feel to

the forests of the Pacific Northwest unlike that of the East Coast, where she spent time in her college days. Fleeting impressions ran through her mind: the shapes of the trees and the scents of the salty sea on the breeze and lush greenery around her. She'd rarely thought about her childhood days here on the island, but now, she felt sure she'd walked this trail before.

She glanced to her left suspiciously. She hadn't heard anything in particular from the shadows on either side of the path, but she felt like something was out there. Taffy would notice if there was anything out in the dark, wouldn't he? He wouldn't continue to play if there was danger. Maybe it was a leftover feeling from a memory.

As she rounded a bend in the trail, she found Taffy standing in a pool of golden light beneath an archway of wisteria. He sat there, his tongue lolled out, looking inordinately pleased with himself.

She sighed. Incorrigible. As she approached, he trotted right through the archway, then bolted. Panic pushed her forward. She didn't want to lose him.

"There's our guest of honor now!" Bridget's voice called out.

A cheer rose up, and Ami pulled up short just through the archway, suddenly faced with a crowd of people. Many were holding drinks and waving. Greetings, expressions of welcome, and encouragements to grab something to eat or drink all blended together into a wall of noise. She wasn't sure how she hadn't heard it before now.

"Good job, Taffy!" Jin's voice carried under the general cacophony.

Det was at her side, not touching her, just a reassuring presence. "Come, enjoy your welcome party."

"Miss Amihan Chanthara, it's a pleasure to meet you."

This new man was the embodiment of tall, sophisticated, and handsome. Black hair fell in careless waves over his deeply brown eyes, but he was saved from a grunge look by having the hair at his nape neatly trimmed. He had pale white skin, a square jaw, and full lips pulled into a close-mouthed smile. When she placed her hand in his, he didn't shake it but instead turned it and brushed cool lips over her knuckles. "I am Sebastian, the host for this evening's festivities and the current mayor of Wolfsound."

"Thank you." Emotions swirled in Ami's gut. She was pleased and self-conscious, touched by the thoughtfulness, and also confused. "It's fine to call me Ami. I'm not sure I'm worth a big fuss."

"Oh but you are," Sebastian insisted, stepping closer. "We're a small community and most people leave for the wider world, but you, your family left and now you've returned. Many of us are delighted. Besides, it's always nice to have a reason for a party here on the island. Indulge us, please."

When he put it that way, and when he leaned toward her with such a charming smile, how could she say no? "I didn't have plans for tonight and Taffy is here somewhere. Thank you."

Det had moved away to sit with Bridget and Jin, the trio having commandeered a table nearby on a raised deck where they could watch the partygoers and gossip. Sebastian was still close, very close.

"Excellent." He smiled. "Why don't we get you something to ea—"

"Here." A plate appeared at her side, delicious aromas wafting up from it. She let her gaze follow the arm attached to the plate, up to the shoulder, and eventually to the face of her benefactor. Lucien looked irritated again—his brows were drawn close together and he was engaging in his favorite hobby of glaring. This time, he was glaring at the town mayor.

Sebastian chuckled, then melted away into the rest of the party. When she didn't say anything, Lucien finally looked at her, and she thought she caught a hint of uncertainty in his silver-grey eyes.

"You don't have to take it if you don't want to," he said finally.

Regret pinged around inside her chest. She hadn't meant to make him feel bad. "I was just caught by surprise."

She took the plate from him. It had seemed small in his hand, but it was wider in diameter than her hand with her fingers fully spread out. There were a variety of bite-sized items, and her mouth watered. She tried what looked like spinach-artichoke dip on a slice of toasted bread first. The creamy richness spread over her tongue, its savoriness contrasted by the bright and herby taste of the marinated artichoke for the perfect balance of salt and vinegar. The bread provided just a bit of crunchy texture.

"The steak slider is medium rare." Lucien still sounded slightly uncomfortable. "I didn't know how you prefer your steak."

"It depends on the cut of steak. I like it so rare it's cool in the middle sometimes, but if it's a marbled cut, I do like it medium rare so the richer parts have a chance to caramelize a little." She picked up a neat bundle of what looked like enoki mushrooms wrapped in super thin slices of seared beef and took a bite. "Mmm. Everything tastes really good. Thank you."

He nodded shortly, hesitated, then seemed to think better of responding and walked away.

She didn't have a chance to wonder if she'd said something wrong because Trey joined her. "Eat up. Those are some choice bites, all great sources of iron."

She smiled at him. That was some random trivia. "I'm glad you're here too."

"Of course. There's plenty of people here, so no need to worry about what nefarious things I might be up to. We're all out in the open." Trey rolled his eyes.

She chuckled and considered her next choice. The selections Lucien had put together on the plate for her really were exceedingly tempting. She decided to try the steak slider next because if it was medium rare, she didn't want it to sit and carry through too far. It turned out to be fork-tender and glorious, complemented perfectly by a generous dollop of creamy, sharp horseradish sauce. The slider roll was perfectly soft and airy, just lightly toasted on the inside.

"Sebastian does put together the best spreads." Trey snagged two glasses of sparkling libation from a tray. "I'll hold yours so you have both hands to eat. Just let me know when you want yours to take a sip."

"You're the best," she said with heartfelt sincerity, then she finished off her steak slider. Even Helen wasn't this perfect a companion. When she and Helen were at a party, it was every person for themselves with the food, and they never came back to a drink either of them might have left unsupervised.

Trey stayed by her side and also held her drink where she could see it at all times. Various people came and introduced themselves. It seemed like the majority of the town was there, but that had to be impossible. The population of the town wasn't huge, but it was at least several thousand, give or take a few dozen. This party was more like a big wedding. There were probably a few hundred in attendance.

It still felt like a lot.

Matsumoto Rio was even there and nodded to Ami just as she was biting into a toast topped with layers of cured salmon with some herby cream cheese mixture piped on top. Ami hurriedly nodded back, but Miss Matsumoto disappeared back into the crowd. Ami breathed a sigh of relief—glad she didn't have to discuss the business proposal she still hadn't opened and reviewed yet—and finished off the second bite of the delicious cured salmon. So good, honestly.

It turned out, the plate Lucien had put together had been just the right amount. Once she'd finished, her hunger had been sated, and she felt comfortably full. She took her drink from Trey and begged off of joining him for a dance for the moment, then wandered away to look for a quiet spot to sit and digest.

There was a short bark, and she turned. She searched the garden area at the edge of the party, which had a view of the harbor leading out to the sound. This was really a lovely space. Taffy?

She found him at the far edge, standing on a large sculpture. "Hey Taffy, this does look like a good spot. Mind if I join you?"

She sat and Taffy jumped down, then rolled onto his back in the thick grass next to her feet.

"Make yourself comfortable," a gravelly, kind voice said from directly under her.

Ami jumped straight up in the air and twisted to face the voice, but her feet weren't as nimble as her mind and she failed to stick her landing, falling backward. She crashed into a firm chest, and strong hands grasped her upper arms, steadying her.

"Easy. He was only being sociable." The voice was familiar, minus the usual irritated drawl.

"He?" Ami was breathless, and her heart raced as she registered the tall, warm body behind her. Lucien.

Legs and a head extended from a large tortoise shell in front of her. A triangular face turned toward her, its slightly hooked jaw moving as words came out. "Hmm. You can call me Genbu."

A low rumbling sound followed, and she realized the tortoise was chuckling. The tortoise. A chuckling, talking tortoise. Had someone managed to slip something into her drink?

"Genbu?" she repeated faintly.

"Clever, yes? I think so, though I've no need for celestial warriors." Genbu planted his sturdy forelimbs into the soft soil of the flower bed and lifted his bulk to turn toward her and Lucien. "So the bookstore has chosen a new Scribe. How has it been treating you?"

How? What? Was it really—?

"Yes, the tortoise is talking. Yes, this is real. Not a prank," Lucien murmured, the heat of his breath tickling her as his lips brushed over the sensitive shell of her ear.

She looked around, but no one else was nearby. Taffy had rolled onto his belly, his hind legs behind him in a relaxed sploot. The tortoise, Genbu, was watching her with glistening, dark eyes, apparently waiting for an answer.

If this was a joke, she'd be playing into it by talking to the tortoise. And this would be proof that Lucien was a jerk. But she hadn't taken Lucien for the type to play elaborate jokes on people. His sense of humor trended toward twisting a person's words and sparring intellectually. This was a prank at a person's expense—not his style.

If her drink had been drugged, then everyone's drinks had been. Trey had taken the drinks from communal serving areas. No one else was stumbling around talking about talking tortoises or any other kinds of hallucinations. She also didn't feel dizzy or disoriented.

She swallowed hard. "Real."

Lucien was warm and real behind her, still steadying her. He whispered his response in her ear. "As improbable as it seems, yeah."

She'd loved folklore and mythology and fairy tales for as long as she could remember. She'd always, always wished magic was real. This wasn't a white rabbit, but she'd go for the adventure.

She thought about the question posed to her. "The bookstore is okay, I think? I've started to explore a little."

"Good." Genbu blinked slowly. "If you put care into the bookstore, it will return what you give it threefold. It needs a Scribe, and you need a new home, I think. It was good to meet you. I'll be going now. Thank you for introducing us, Taffy."

Taffy stood and woofed softly, then stretched his neck forward until he booped noses with the tortoise.

She waited, watching the tortoise walk away and disappear into the hedges. Lucien's heart beat slow and steady against her back. His hands dropped from her arms and he stepped away. The cool night air touched her back, and she missed his warmth. No one jumped out to laugh or tell her it had all been a gag.

"That was real." She craned her neck to find Lucien still nearby, just standing at arm's length.

He nodded. "There's more to this world than most

humans realize, particularly here on this island. There was some debate about whether you needed to know or not. I guess Genbu made an executive decision."

"Executive," she breathed. "Is he in charge, then?"

"He's the oldest of the supernatural community here." Lucien shrugged. "There are several old powers living on the island. They mostly like to observe and gossip and leave the onerous responsibilities of leadership to some of us relatively younger leaders."

She stared at him. He was a leader? Of who?

She wrapped her arms around herself, then rubbed her upper arms where his hands had been. Her skin still tingled from his touch. "Whether I needed to know. I guess not all humans know then."

"Astute deduction." His snark was back.

"And this is about the bookstore?" She had been wondering why she'd felt so comfortable there. Despite faint childhood memories of it, it was an unfamiliar place. Yet anytime she thought of looking for something or had a need, she'd experience a sort of hunch and know just where to find it. It was subtle, hard to put into words. It had felt silly to ask even herself, but now she voiced the question aloud, "Is it magic?"

Lucien nodded. "The simple answer is yes. You're probably going to want a more detailed explanation, so let me stop you right there. I don't know the full extent of what it does. I never spent much time in there anyway, and any interaction I've had with either the bookstore or you in the last day or two wasn't planned."

That last sentence splashed her like cold water. She didn't particularly want to examine why either, not at the moment.

"So you're not human?" She asked the question as an

experiment, to find out if he would still answer any questions at all, if he had the answers to them.

He was quiet long enough that she looked up at him. His face was almost a blank mask, and his eyes caught the moonlight. As her gaze met with his, he uttered one word. "No."

Ah. Well. How did she feel about that? Curiosity had been the initial driver, but it would make sense if she experienced some kind of recoil. Wouldn't it?

"I'll save you the trouble of asking the obvious follow-up question: I'm a werewolf." His revelation was delivered in a flat tone.

She resisted the urge to let her gaze travel down his body, looking for visible signs. She knew she wouldn't find any. She'd ogled him plenty today on the way to and from lunch, and yesterday too. He was an undeniably attractive man and no, she'd had no idea he was anything other than human.

His blank expression melted slightly, and he raised that damn eyebrow at her again. "You're not afraid."

"Should I be?" Okay, maybe she hadn't meant to sound as exasperated as she did. Now that the question was out of her mouth, it was obvious she should be, unless she was too stupid to live.

How about cautious? Wary. Both of those seemed a reasonable compromise.

He smirked. "Fear would be the more popular reaction for those who find out."

"I just met a talking tortoise. I live in a magic building," she said. Her brain was popping words directly into her mouth without giving her much of a chance to process what she was saying. "Maybe I'll be afraid in a little while, after I catch up with it all."

THE INK THAT BLEEDS

He remained silently staring at her.

A shiver ran over her skin. She still wasn't afraid. Instead, she wanted to step closer to him. Wanted to know why he was here, with her.

"Does it happen often? People finding out?" Questions were piling up in her head, and it was easier to press forward with those than linger on how he made her feel. She wished she had her traveler's notebook with her. Her fingers twitched as she ached for her favorite fountain pen.

"No." He paused. "No, it doesn't happen often. And to be clear, no, you needn't be afraid. Not of me."

Warmth bloomed low in her belly again. "I have a lot of questions."

He chuckled. "I imagine so. There's not enough time in the night to answer them all."

"But I can ask them?" She almost took a step toward him but stopped. Before he could answer, she added, "and you'll answer?"

He closed his mouth, pressing his lips together in a thin line for a beat. "I'll answer some. I won't promise to answer everything, but I'll answer what I can."

She rocked back on her heels. "That's fair."

More than fair.

"There you are!" Mel came striding over, stepping right into Ami's space. "I'm off duty. Will you dance with me?"

Ami blushed. "Maybe not tonight."

Mel cocked their head to one side. "All right. Maybe another time?"

The question held more than a request to dance, Ami thought. Mel's face was flushed, and there was no denying they were attractive. But Mel was close right now, and their proximity didn't set off the fluttery excitement Ami had been experiencing even a few seconds ago while Lucien had been standing an arm's length away. The chemistry was incomparable.

"Maybe a friendly dance, next time." Ami made direct eye contact as she answered, keeping her tone steady and gentle.

Mel's mouth twisted into a rueful smile and their eyes darted toward Lucien, then returned to Ami. "Friends. Absolutely. Have you had fun getting acquainted with people tonight?"

They stepped back a little and turned their body to include Lucien in the conversation.

Ami gave them a grateful smile in return. "It's been enlightening."

Lucien chuckled. "Genbu decided to introduce himself to her earlier."

Mel's eyebrows almost disappeared into their hairline. "Well, then. Welcome to a very exclusive club. Unless you aren't human either. Are you human?"

Lucien glanced at the glass in Mel's hand. "How much have you had to drink?"

"A little more than usual." Mel waved their free hand at Lucien in dismissal. "This isn't an easy case and it's my first murder. I've got multiple possible suspects, no real idea of how the murder was committed, and pressure from the town to make an arrest so people feel safe again."

"You've had too much—" Lucien started, but stopped as Ami gave him a pointed look.

"I'd really appreciate knowing more about how Nancy died, if you can share with me," Ami said quietly. No one else was nearby. "I'd rest easier if I knew what happened to her."

For a lot of reasons, not just because Nancy had been her predecessor.

"Well, like I said, you're part of a rather private club," Mel said, stepping closer. Their hand shot out and snagged Lucien by the sleeve, then dragged him closer too. Once the three of them were in a tight huddle, Mel took a steadying breath. "All right. On the day of Nancy's death, she had an argument with her ex-boyfriend early in the day. There were witnesses once the fight spilled out of the bookstore onto the main street. Trey was involved."

"Ah." Ami had been wondering.

Trey said he'd been a regular at the bookstore. It could've been a coincidence. Lucien didn't seem to think Trey had been guilty of anything related to Nancy's death.

"So there's two of our suspects right there. I'm still going through both Trey's statement and the ex-boyfriend's," Mel continued. "Later in the day, Nancy also had a strained disagreement with Matsumoto Rio at the Thai restaurant."

Which explained why Lucien had been wary of the woman when she'd shown up at the bookstore earlier in the day. Ami really wished she had her traveler's journal now.

"Was the fire at the bookstore related?" Lucien asked.

Mel lifted a shoulder and dropped it. "Possibly. The fire was put out before there was any real damage, but Nancy was missing. Very suspicious. Nancy's body washed up on shore the next morning with high tide, sometime before dawn."

Wow. It was a lot of information to absorb.

Lucien muttered, "Why do I need to be a part of this little briefing?"

"Because I was going to ask for your help anyway." Mel grinned at him. "Not sure if you've had a chance to let Ami here know about the heightened senses you have, being a werewolf and all that. You've got the super-olfactory advantage and the extra-sharp vision. We don't have a K9 unit on the island and you're my next best resource. We can call you a special consultant."

Ami clapped her hand over her mouth before she laughed. It wasn't the blithe way Mel had delivered their reasoning. It was the look of absolute indignation on Lucien's face. She was very glad she was there to witness it.

CHAPTER

FIVE

P eace had finally returned to the sound in the late hours between midnight and dawn, and Lucien was grateful. It wasn't ever truly quiet, not this close to the water. Waves crashed into the rocky shore at this portion of the bay. Winds came off the bay and sang through the open canopy of the forest—a mix of Douglas fir, Sitka spruce, big-leaf maple, and western red cedar. He loved it here on the island, with its unique mix of woods and sea.

The town elders had ensured many of the native species remained as well: western hemlock, grand fir, Pacific yew, and shore pine. The longer-lived denizens recognized the value of preserving the life on and around this place, and he respected that. It was drier on the islands than the nearby mainland, so these woods had little undergrowth compared to the lush green that grew around the base of the trees on the mainland. It made it easier for him to run through the woods, whether he was in wolf or human form, or the rarer meld of both.

Officially, there were no large predators running

through the forests on the islands either. But he had been born and raised here, a part of a small pack. He'd learned how to hide his presence in the trees early on and to blend with the humans in town at the same time.

"Thank you for returning in such a timely manner." Sebastian's voice floated out from the dark.

Lucien shrugged. He could have come back earlier, but the party hadn't completely wound down until just an hour ago and Sebastian often lingered with his last few guests. Lucien wasn't in a position to judge another predator, so long as Sebastian wasn't torturing anyone. The vampire had made it clear he followed a moral code of sorts, and Lucien would respect it, for now.

"The bookstore's new Scribe is quite charming." Sebastian came to stand next to Lucien, looking out over the water with him.

It was easier for them both to have a common view to enjoy during their talks. Direct eye contact incited their predatory instincts, and it was hard enough for two types of apex predators to exist on the island, let alone work together, as they were expected to.

"She's off limits." Lucien tried to keep the growl out of his voice, but when it came anyway, he wasn't particularly sorry.

"You made that clear earlier." Sebastian chuckled. "No worries. I recognize your prior claim."

Lucien frowned. He hadn't intended to make a claim either, but that might not be worth clarifying with the vampire. If he went out of his way to deny it, Sebastian might perceive room for opportunity. Best to leave it alone. He hadn't taken much time to really think about why he'd been looking out for her tonight anyway. Maybe it was because she'd befriended Trey so readily, even after she knew Trey was considered a person of interest in the case.

Trey was from the mainland and was still settling into the pack. He found it easier to make friends among the human portion of the population. Amihan was now someone who could know Trey was a werewolf, and their friendship could form with open honesty in that regard. Lucien had that with Mel and it made a difference.

Lucien couldn't help Trey navigate the challenges of romantic relationships, mostly because Lucien was dodging those himself. Easier to focus on taking over leadership responsibilities within his pack. Ensuring close to a dozen werewolves could safely live in close proximity to humans and remain peacefully integrated into the island community was enough to occupy his days and nights. It wasn't a good time for distraction, no matter how attractive she was.

"She's from the island. I'm not sure how much she remembers, but it isn't much." It was a source of much of his frustration when it came to Amihan. "We were classmates in primary school. Rivals, of a sort. She doesn't recognize me or Mel."

It bothered him that she didn't recognize him. As if their years of competing for top grades had been nothing, when to the child he was, beating her academic scores had meant everything.

"Oh?" Sebastian's glance slanted in Lucien's direction. "When was this?"

Werewolves could live a lot longer than humans, if they could survive. It was a reasonable question since Lucien's childhood could have been far longer ago than most humans would have imagined. But Amihan was human, and he was relatively young, as werewolves went. "This was a little over twenty years ago. We were twelve when her family left the island."

There had been an accident. Lucien was glad she didn't remember that. He would never forget it, never stop regretting the choice he'd made. How he'd failed.

"Ah, so during one of my periods of absence." Sebastian lifted his hand to tap a finger at his lips.

"I think Bennett was here to carry on the family tradition while you were gone," Lucien grumbled.

Sebastian nodded. "Indeed. He is based rather locally without the desire to take over this particular territory permanently. And he has demonstrated the ability to work with other supernaturals rather effectively, werewolves included."

Lucien grunted. The werewolf working for the Darke Consortium, Thomas, was more of a loner than any from Lucien's pack. "That Bennett and Thomas could work together was nothing short of a wonder of nature and that isn't as much about what they are so much as who they are."

"Hah. True." Sebastian shifted his stance slightly. "It is a good thing there is another of my kind nearby willing to both take on the responsibilities of the island for a few decades and cede leadership back to me when I return."

"If you say so." Lucien crossed his arms. "Politics are more your thing. The humans on the island definitely like to vote one of you into office as the generations come and go. Must be the charisma that comes with being one of your kind."

Sebastian chuckled. "It is amusing to leave and come back as my own nephew or grandson. My constituents love a family legacy."

"Yeah well, while you were gone that time, there was an

incident. Amihan was caught up in it." Lucien had to consciously ease the tension in his jaw. "Her parents spooked and decided to move back to the mainland. I think Bennett took measures to ensure none of them thought much about anyone here."

It wasn't memory tampering, per se. The muse, Asamoah, had the ability to inspire or suppress the likelihood of thoughts, ideas, or memories occurring to a person. It was formidable when used the way it had been on people leaving Wolfsound. As they went on with their lives, thoughts of the island and their time there just didn't occur to those people again.

"It would have been a prudent precaution," Sebastian agreed. "Now that she's back, I assume you are wondering if her memories will return?"

Lucien hesitated, then admitted, "I don't know whether I want them to or not. If the bookstore has chosen her, and I'm only just learning about what the bookstore is, then Amihan is now a key member of the supernatural community. She falls under our protection. I remember my history with her, which makes it complicated for me, and irritates me. That's not quite fair to her."

"Perhaps it would be better if I was the primary liaison with the bookstore's Scribe, then." Concern laced Sebastian's tone.

"No." His rejection of Sebastian's suggestion was a visceral reaction. There had been a lot of wolf in his voice there.

"Get your head right, wolf." Sebastian's tone had sharpened. "A werewolf cannot afford to ride his temper around humans. They are too delicate. If you cannot resolve this irritation, this frustration, you need to step back and let one of us be her shield."

If he stepped back, then he would be ceding the field to Amihan. Even if she didn't recall their childhood rivalry, he did. And the adult she was now didn't hesitate to stand up to him, challenge him. He refused to let her win, even in this small way.

"I've got this." Lucien was firm in his decision. "Besides, Mel has asked both me and Amihan to serve as special consultants to the police for this investigation. It's not like you can make yourself available to work with either of them."

Not during daylight hours. It was enough that the mayor's office only ever held office hours in the late evening, ostensibly to make them more available to the townspeople without interfering with day jobs. Forcing the sheriff's investigational activities to also occur at night would be more than the humans of the town would believe practical.

The vampire hissed. Lucien smiled into the night but didn't say anything to provoke the vampire further. At least, not for the moment.

"How much support are we providing to human law enforcement in regard to the investigation of the death of the former bookstore owner?" Sebastian asked. The vampire's tone had shifted to gentle inquisitiveness.

Lucien crossed his arms over his chest. Nancy Greene had been one of the repeated consenting donors to Sebastian, another reason Lucien had tensed up when Sebastian approached Amihan at the party. But to his knowledge, Nancy had offered. Sebastian had not proposed the . . . understanding between Nancy and Sebastian.

Lucien sighed. Give him a fresh rabbit or deer any day.

"I'll do what I can to aid the investigation." Even if he had to stand in for a K9 unit. Lucien was not going to forgive Mel for that comparison anytime soon. "That includes gathering information on any known associates of Nancy's."

Like Sebastian.

"I would be happy to give you and the sheriff a statement of my whereabouts the evening of the murder." All semblance of banter or warmth had gone from Sebastian's tone.

"Do you have a solid alibi?" Lucien's understanding of terminology used in formal investigations was limited, but he at least knew that an account of the person's whereabouts at the time a crime was committed was a key piece of required information.

"No." Sebastian sounded weary now. "I understand what that means. However, I had no reason to cause Nancy undue harm. In fact, my understanding with her would indicate I had a vested interest in her ongoing well-being. Consenting humans, who are not overcome with delusions of eternal youth, are rather hard to come by."

Lucien nodded. It was a reasonable rationale, for supernaturals. It would be harder to justify in a human police report, unless they were able to identify a much more likely suspect. Ideally, they needed to apprehend the actual murderer.

"You know where to find me when you need an official statement." Sebastian turned to leave, then paused. "I would be interested to know if this death was about Nancy or about the bookstore."

"I'll find out," Lucien said.

He'd made the commitment more for Amihan, and himself, than out of any commitment to the vampire.

◊

"THESE ARE HUMAN TREATS," Ami explained to Taffy as she used a folded hand towel to pull a tray out of the oven. "Let me do some research to figure out how to bake dog-safe treats later, if there's not a shop that specializes in those somewhere in town."

As soon as she placed the baking tray on top of the stove to cool, she jotted the task on a sticky note and stuck it inside her traveler's notebook to take downstairs and put on her kanban board behind the counter. Keeping all her to-do notes downstairs was a part of her new habit strategy. She wanted to keep her living space soothing, without any to-do lists in any form anywhere. So far, it was a huge improvement. She found herself much more relaxed in her own private spaces than she had in years.

Day three on this island, and she was already slowly breaking her need to have her phone in hand every moment. Tasks could wait downstairs in the bookstore for when she was ready to start work for the day. She was not going to recover from burnout by being mentally in work-mode twenty-four hours a day, seven days a week.

Task safely tucked away so she wouldn't be anxious about forgetting it, she turned back to her baked goods. She used a fork to carefully tip them out of the baking tins and pierce them to let out steam. They'd turned out perfectly. Ami did a little happy dance in her kitchen at the success of her first experimental bake using an unfamiliar oven.

"Welcome back to the world of the actively living, Fred."

Stress baking—or stress cooking—was a key part of her burnout recovery plan. It made her equally as happy to feed friends. She smiled as she thought about it. She was making friends here, something she'd hoped for but hadn't let herself set as an expectation.

She glanced at her phone on the breakfast table to check the time. The only notifications she allowed on-screen were texts from Helen, and there was one waiting for her.

You're baking, aren't you?

Ami sent her best friend a quick picture of the sourdough popovers she'd just pulled out of the oven.

Mmm yes. Tell me Mr. Naughty is visiting today. Feed the man!

Ami picked up her phone and typed out a reply. *Yes, he's going to be here, with the town sheriff. This is official police business. I'm just baking for us all while we work together. That's all.*

Helen must have been between meetings because her response came back fast.

Thou dost give too much explanation. It'll keep him coming back. You want him to come.

Another text came from Helen almost immediately.

Admit it! You want him to come.

Ami glared at her phone. There was no need for the eggplant emojis. Absolutely . . .

She felt rather than heard the knock at the front door and swiftly tapped the text notification to clear it from her screen. Taffy scampered to the bottom of the stairs, glanced back to be sure she was coming, then went ahead of her to greet whoever was here.

Lucien and Mel were waiting when she opened the front door.

Mel entered and tapped the new sign Ami had placed in one of the display windows to replace the Open or Closed sign. This one read

CLOSED

. . . but reopening soon!

"Smart!" Mel grinned.

Ami shrugged. "Yesterday seemed to be a day for telling people I wasn't ready to open the bookstore yet."

Lucien nodded to her. "Amihan."

Annoyance sparked in her chest, along with that fluttering feeling she didn't want to think about. "Lucien. Any reason you persist in using my entire given name, rather than the nickname everyone else uses?"

"Quite possibly the same reason you use mine."

Fine then.

Ami studied him for a moment. He had dark circles under his eyes, which didn't take anything away from his handsome face overall—especially if you went for the brooding, grumpy look. But it seemed different from how he'd looked over the past couple of days.

"Have you already eaten? Need caffeine? I've got coffee upstairs, or tea, if you prefer." Even if they'd already had breakfast, she offered out of habit. It was a thing in her parents' household to make sure no guest went hungry. She wanted to do the same. Besides, she had been about to have second breakfast anyway. It tasted better shared.

"I will never say no to coffee." Mel headed toward the stairs leading down into the basement level of the bookstore. "We planned to take over the reading room downstairs. It can work as a conference room and the police station doesn't have a space for this kind of collaborative work with sensitive information."

Lucien simply followed Mel. He paused as he passed Ami. "Coffee would be good, thanks."

"Did you get any sleep last night?" she asked.

His response was another grunt.

He'd still been at the party when she'd left around midnight. Trey had told her those parties could go for hours longer, which was why she hadn't tried to last to the end even if she was the guest of honor. She'd started to fade as early as ten.

She met them all the way downstairs with her sleek tech backpack on her back and a tray in her hands. The tray was loaded with a pot of coffee, her hot water heater, some loose tea for herself, and mugs for all. She'd also placed a basket of her morning baking on the tray alongside dishes full of butter and jam. She placed the tray on the sideboard at one end of the small reading room and plugged in her hot water heater. She considered ordering a second one to have down here all the time. She'd add it to her list of future updates to the bookstore.

"Something smells amazing." Mel was spreading a few folios of documents across the table in the middle of the room.

Lucien was opening up a laptop. "Good thing we can still get signal down here. We can hotspot off my phone."

"I set up Wi-Fi last night." Ami unlocked her phone and brought up the appropriate digital note, then slid it across the table to Lucien. "There's one for guests of the bookstore and a secured one for private use."

The note she'd displayed on her phone was for the secure Wi-Fi. She'd done research before arriving and come prepared to set it up as soon as possible. She might be developing better work-life balance habits, but she wanted internet connectivity for quality of life. Lucien didn't comment, just tapped briefly at his laptop.

Ami shook her head, mildly irritated for no good reason. But would it kill him to acknowledge her efficiency? "There's fresh sourdough popovers here, if you're hungry. I woke up Fred yesterday, got some basic pantry supplies in the afternoon, and wanted to get acquainted with the oven."

Lucien shot a look at her but turned away before she could ask him what his problem was. He slid her phone back across the tabletop to her.

Another text notification from Helen was there on-screen.

Did Mr. Naughty come yet???

Ami bit her lip and snatched her phone up from the table to clear the notification.

"Fred?" Mel joined her at the side counter.

"My sourdough starter. I brought it with me as dried flakes. It doesn't take much to reconstitute and feed to bring it back to life." Ami shrugged. "The popovers were a way to put the discard to good use. The recipe doesn't require particularly active sourdough starter. It'll take a few days before Fred is frisky enough to make bread."

Lucien was back to watching her, this time with a quizzical expression.

"What?" She wondered how he managed to get her defensive without even saying anything. She was letting him get under her skin.

He only shook his head. "There's just a lot going on in your head and sometimes it's like information comes out of you like fresh-popped popcorn out of a movie theater popper."

Mel snickered, their mouth full of buttered popover slathered in jam. "He's not wrong."

Ami huffed and shoved a mug of coffee in front of him. "Try it first before you assume you need cream and sugar."

She'd always assumed coffee needed at least sugar, if not a generous amount of creamer, until she'd learned to brew pour-over. Now, she invested in good beans and put the extra couple of minutes into grinding and brewing her coffee. She saved her sugar intake for her baking.

Mel carried their mug and a second loaded popover to the table. "S'good."

"So, I figure we can use this wall to mind map as we go." Ami pulled out packs of various colored sticky notes from her backpack.

She also pulled out her travel fountain pen case and traveler's notebook, then opened to a completely new insert so she could pull it out and hand it over to Mel, if necessary. Then she placed her laptop and a digital tablet on the table, complete with wireless styluses. In minutes, she had her laptop open to a word processing app and had the tablet configured to act as a secondary display.

Mel was staring at her. "You bake, play with pens and planners, and use more technology than me and Lucien combined. Any other superpowers?"

Lucien stood, went to the sideboard, and helped himself to a popover.

"Well, I thought about what skills I have to help, since you told me you were going to get Lucien to act as a special consultant for you." Ami could have just given them the space to work, but she admitted to herself it would have killed her to just go back upstairs and go about the day, tweaking things around the bookstore. She'd been included in the conversation, and she was curious about the case, so if she could contribute value, she wanted to be involved. "I spent ten years in project management, task prioritization, and business process design. I'm experienced in facilitating strategy or planning sessions and running brainstorming workshops. At the very least, I'm a detail-oriented note-taker. I hoped you'd let me help."

Her phone had also never been off. Her email inbox had received hundreds, sometimes thousands of emails a day, and she'd kept the unread number at zero. She'd worked fifty- and sixty-hour workweeks on a regular basis, often going to eighty hours at key phases of any given project. She'd come here to change the pace of her life before she damaged herself permanently. But she couldn't give it all up completely.

This would be a way for her to ease herself out of her old life and still exercise parts of her mind in which she took a lot of pride.

Lucien returned to his seat and tapped one of the documents. "Let's get started, then."

Mel smiled at Ami and opened the first set of documents. "Here's the list of people who had any kind of contact with the victim the day of or within two weeks of her death."

SIX

L ucien glared at the sea of sticky notes on the wall in the tiny reading room. "We need to narrow down the suspect list."

"This is why I said I needed help," Mel moaned.

To be fair, Amihan had neatly organized all of the potential suspects with multiple visual cues to help them make sense of the masses.

"On the bright side, I'm guessing the bookstore gets a lot of foot traffic." Amihan stood with her hands on her hips, staring at the wall. "Really, this is a result of broad parameters. We can prioritize to just a handful right away and focus the actual investigative activities on those first, and save the rest for secondary and tertiary effort if none of the initial leads make sense."

Mel blinked owlishly. "How are you picking out just a handful?"

Lucien crossed his arms and leaned back. He had it down to a dozen, but he was interested in what Amihan would suggest.

"See these ones here? They're the only people who

had an actual two-way conversation with the victim the day of the murder or in the days leading up to it, either verbally or via some type of electronic communication like email or text. Nancy actually communicated back and forth with them. That's why they're on orange sticky notes." Amihan pulled several sticky notes and relocated them to the top of their little flock on the wall.

Amihan continued, "Plus, they were part of some sort of disagreement involving Nancy, either directly or were sucked into the discussion tangentially. That's why I wrote their names with the oxblood-colored ink. There's only three of them."

Paper-color and ink-color organization. How many fountain pens did she own? On the other hand, if he ever wanted to give her a gift, he knew what to get her. Not that he had any reason to be gifting her anything.

Lucien scowled, yanking his errant thoughts back on task. "Isn't that narrowing down the field too far?"

Amihan shook her head. "It's a place to start. We can focus our investigation on them and eliminate them from the potential-suspects list right away. Sort of a fail-fast approach."

Mel hummed appreciatively as they continued to study the wall of information. "I like the idea of prioritizing who we talk to, but I'm not sure I understand exactly what you mean by fail-fast approach."

Amihan practically bounced on the balls of her feet as she explained. "Motive, opportunity, means, alibi. If any of these conditions isn't met, we have an immediate indicator of failure to qualify for further investigation. It's not exactly the ideal of innocent until proven guilty, but it does prove someone isn't guilty quicker. If we eliminate all three from the potential-suspects list, we move to tier 2 persons of interest."

Lucien resisted the urge to grin as he watched her. There was a warmth blooming in his chest and it had to be heartburn from eating too many of her popovers. It had nothing to do with how she lit up the room with her enthusiasm or how blindingly fast that mind of hers worked. Nothing to do with any of that.

She snagged another handful of sticky notes. Some of these were orange but a couple were not. They were all written on in different ink colors too. He'd thought she'd been fickle, switching from pen to pen as they'd gone through the information. Now, he realized with a slowly growing admiration, her methodic note-taking was allowing for a speedy analysis of the data they'd reviewed.

Her mind was impressive, and a little scary.

Mel stretched their arms above their head, then let out a slow sigh. "This feels a lot more approachable now."

Amihan nodded. "It definitely overcomes analysis paralysis to prioritize like this. We're not overlooking anyone, just prioritizing how we go through them in the most efficient way. I'm guessing time might be a consideration too. Until we know why the victim was murdered, we don't know if it's a one-time thing."

Lucien looked at Amihan sharply. It had been almost imperceptible, but her voice had wobbled on that last statement. Was she afraid? If she was, he hadn't smelled a hint of it from her.

She was much too good at bottling up her emotions. He wondered if it was from years of managing meetings with difficult personalities trapped for way too long in stuffy boardrooms. No wonder she had burned out. Anyone who threw this much of their soul into making certain a given effort was successful would. She didn't keep much back for herself.

"I think it's time for lunch." He decided both Mel and Amihan needed more substantial food than light and fluffy carbs slathered in butter and sugary preserves, no matter how good they'd tasted. Taffy had given up on all three of them and was snoozing under the table, where he was safe from being trampled as Amihan moved back and forth in front of her sticky note mind map on the wall.

"Yeah." Mel stood. "Then I think you can leave formal interrogation to me. Lucien will apply his particular skills to visiting each of their homes."

Amihan nodded.

Lucien kept his groan to himself. He wasn't looking forward to visiting anyone. Trey, at least, knew what Lucien was, so there was no need to be subtle. The other two would require a more circumspect approach, which he could do, but it took energy.

The three of them walked together out of the bookstore, Taffy at Amihan's heels.

When they arrived at the Thai restaurant, they spotted Trey alone in a booth. Amihan lifted her chin in greeting, a quick upward head nod, and he smiled back and motioned for them to join him.

"Awkward," Mel muttered. "I guess I could ask him to come with me to the station after we finish lunch. We can make it discreet."

"That'd be appreciated, Mel." Lucien kept his voice pitched low too. The townsfolk liked to chatter and connect the dots with their own assumptions. The fewer rumors about any of his pack members, the better.

Amihan had slid into the booth opposite Trey, leaving the two outside seats for Mel and Lucien. Lucien narrowed his eyes at Amihan, wondering if she'd anticipated the two of them wanting the positions that would allow them to get to their feet the quickest. She seemed oblivious to his scrutiny, animatedly talking about ink and fountain pens with Trey.

Det arrived to take their order personally. Amihan brought her hands together in greeting, a gesture Det returned, then gave her order in Thai. The usually stone-faced serpent actually had a ghost of a smile playing around his thin lips as he spoke to her. Interesting.

"I apologize if it's rude," she said to all of them. "I jump at the chance to practice whenever I can. I don't want to lose the language."

Mel only shrugged with a smile and Trey leaned forward. "I think it's great. So you're Thai then?"

"Half." Amihan smiled. "I was born here. My mother is Thai and my father is Filipino, both second-generation diaspora. They live on the East Coast now. I speak a bit of Tagalog too. But I'm better at speaking Thai, mostly because I watch a lot of Thai dramas from my mom's recommendations. She's always sending me links to the ones she's watching."

"I love Asian dramas," Trey gushed. "So much angst and shenanigans. Seriously."

"Yes!" Amihan leaned forward. "Korean dramas are my favorite. They're so good at bringing up all the feels. Does anything happen like that in real life?"

Mel shook their head. "Here on the island? No."

Lucien was not participating in this conversation.

"I don't know." Trey tipped his head to one side. "Maybe it's not right to get into it, but the day before Nancy . . . left us, I got caught up in some real drama between her and her ex-boyfriend."

Amihan's eyes went wide. "No."

Encouraged, Trey lowered his voice to a conspiratorial whisper. "Okay, yes. And it's probably something that'll come up in the investigation, so it's not like it's a secret, but her and her ex had parted ways already."

"Already broke up?" Amihan asked, sitting up straight with interest.

Lucien bit back another grin. He was doing that a lot today.

Trey nodded. "But that morning, he came back and proposed."

"No," Amihan breathed, sounding a little bit horrified.

"Yes." Trey placed a hand flat on the tabletop. "When she told him it was over, he did *not* take it well. I happened to be at the bookstore at the time and he started throwing stuff around, knocking books off the shelves and having an all-out temper tantrum. When Nancy told him he needed to get out, I felt I needed to back her up because I didn't want him to actually hit her."

Amihan was listening intently. Mel had stilled and caught Lucien's gaze. This was exactly the candid information they needed. It added context to why Trey had been involved in the fight other people had witnessed that day. Trey had been too stressed out to explain when Lucien had asked him about it earlier.

But here he was, sharing with Amihan. If Mel asked him about it in a formal interview, all they needed to do was check for consistency. Lucien didn't smell or see any physical tells of deception. Trey was sharing the truth and, while it didn't clear him, it provided a reasonable explanation for his involvement.

"Wow." Amihan shuddered. "Yeah, I feel very thankful I've got no toxic exes to worry about."

Lucien was insanely pleased to hear that and he really had no reason to care.

"Yeah, I was so shaken, I couldn't finish the K-drama I've been watching." Trey scratched the back of his neck. "I ended up binging a totally different drama, a wuxia, all night. I looked out and saw the dawn and realized I got no sleep at all."

Amihan laughed. "I've done that. I look up and realize how much time went by, like oops! What streaming service do you use? Some of them even log the time you've spent watching, or after a while, they pop up with that message asking whether you want to keep watching, yes or no. I feel so judged."

"Right?" Trey laughed.

Lucien realized Amihan had given Mel and him another way to establish Trey's alibi, despite him having been alone all night during the time of the murder. Mel could request log-in information to confirm he'd been actively streaming.

It was hard to believe she was doing it on purpose and it wasn't a formal interrogation.

"Don't you have a bookstore to run?"

Ami rolled her eyes at Lucien's tone. She was starting to learn the difference between when he was being a complete jerk and when he was just a little grumpy. That question was definitely grump. "Mel is doing the formal interview with Trey to take down his statement related to the case. It doesn't make sense for me to be a part of that. But I do have a business proposal from Matsumoto Rio and it would make sense for me to pay her a visit, which gives you a reason to be there. We can stop by the bookstore and pick it up."

"I fail to understand how your reason for being there has anything to do with me." Lucien sounded irritable, but he did shorten his strides so she didn't have to hop-skip every few steps to keep up with him. The man had long, long legs.

It took less than a few minutes to pop into the bookstore, grab a few things, and leave Taffy to guard the store. Or at least, that's what she told Taffy when she explained why he couldn't come along. It was one thing to take Taffy with her to the public places around town. Almost all of them were pet-friendly. But they would be going to someone's private residence.

They were on their way shortly, and Lucien hadn't stopped scowling the entire time.

"So what were you going to do? Just knock on the door and demand Miss Matsumoto allow you in to sniff around the house? Literally?" Ami tried lifting her eyebrow in his direction. He just honestly used it to better effect. She pressed on. "You were with me when Miss Matsumoto dropped off the proposal at the bookstore. You were even sort of grr, rawr! at her. It wouldn't be all that odd for you to also show up when I came to discuss it."

Lucien remained silent, but he continued at a pace conducive to an easy walk for her.

After a moment, he muttered, "I was not all grr, rawr."

She smothered a giggle. He had been, though. Miss Matsumoto hadn't backed away or acted overtly intimidated in any way, but Ami had a decent amount of experience reading the body language of people from a variety of cultures. Matsumoto Rio had withdrawn and taken care not to project any movement or posture that might escalate the situation. She'd been wary.

Lucien pivoted to face her suddenly—so quickly, she walked right into him. She face planted right into the center of his chest, and as she stumbled back, his hands grasped her elbows to steady her. She looked up into his face, startled.

He looked down at her, and his grey eyes lightened to silver. "When I growl at you, you'll know."

His voice was so deep, so dark, delightful shivers ran through her. She opened and closed her mouth, unable to come up with any kind of response.

He smirked at her and shifted his body, giving her room to breathe, then jerked his head to one side. "We're here. Just head up this walkway to the house. We'll go with your plan and I'll be your . . . escort, for this visit."

Be still her beating heart. No. Really. Her heart needed to calm down or she might not make it through the next couple of minutes, much less a discussion with a complete stranger about a business proposal related to a property Ami had only just inherited.

The walkway he indicated ran alongside a curving driveway and down a short lane of trees to a house set back and away from the street. It wasn't a huge property, but it had been landscaped to provide privacy. They walked up to the front door, and it opened smoothly, as if Matsumoto Rio had known they were coming.

Well, there had been plenty of opportunity to notice them walking up the drive.

"Miss Chanthara, Mister Allard, welcome." Matsumoto Rio wore a decidedly neutral expression as she gave a shallow bow from the hips, the ends of her hair falling forward to brush her jawline. Her hair was so black, but also had blue and purple highlights in it, contrasting the pearl paleness of her skin with its warm golden undertone. "Your visit is unexpected."

"We apologize for coming without calling ahead." Ami knew it was rude but better to show up unannounced than give any of the persons of interest time to hide anything. Next to her, Lucien remained silent. "I had hoped to get to know you a little better and perhaps ask a few questions now that I've had a chance to read through your business proposal."

"Of course." Their host stepped back and motioned for them to enter. Her tone was quiet and even. It wasn't particularly cold, but she wasn't welcoming either.

The entryway had a small shoe rack to one side, and a pair of slippers was placed neatly a little farther into the home. Ami entered, making certain not to step past the slippers with her outdoor shoes. She bent to place her shoes neatly on the shoe rack. After a moment's hesitation, Lucien did the same.

"I have only recently moved here, so I do not have guest slippers to offer you."

Ami shook her head, smiling. "Oh, please don't worry. I've also brought a small gift, as an apology for coming unexpectedly."

Ami pulled a small container out of her backpack. She hadn't had a chance to do more than wrap it in a cute kitchen towel. She hoped it looked at least somewhat nice. "It's kanom mor kaeng, one of my favorite desserts. I made it with mung beans, eggs, and coconut milk, with a little palm sugar, but not much, so it's not too sweet."

"Thank you, Miss Chanthara." She still didn't seem to be warming up to them. In fact, Matsumoto Rio seemed to be ignoring Lucien.

Fine. Ami could keep up the kindness until everyone in the room drowned in it. "Oh, call me Ami, please."

"Ami." Their host blinked liquid brown eyes so dark, they were almost black. "Then please use my given name also."

There was a hint of warmth. Ami almost bounced on the balls of her feet. "Thank you, Rio."

Rio's mouth might have curved into a ghost of a smile, maybe. It was hard to tell. Suddenly, they were headed deeper into the house, moving faster than Ami could track visually. "Would you like tea?"

In moments, they were seated around a round table nestled into a breakfast nook with windows looking out onto a small yard. Rio had poured hot tea for Ami and herself. Lucien had a glass of ice water, at his request. Pieces of the kanom mor kaeng had been served on small plates with tiny, slender two-tined dessert forks.

Ami fidgeted, embarrassed at how clumsy she felt. She had expressed curiosity about everything and anything around the home to give herself and Lucien a chance to walk over and take a look at it. But there wasn't much. The home was arranged in an almost-minimalist style.

"What other questions can I answer for you?" Rio asked finally. She sounded exasperated.

Nothing left to ask about but the business proposal. Ami took the papers out of their envelope. They had a variety of the clear sticky notes she liked to use when she wanted to make annotations but didn't want to write on the original documents.

"I'm actually a little confused about the main goal." Ami placed her hands on the pages as she spoke. "Initially, I thought this was an offer to buy the bookstore, but as I read the second and third pages, I realized it might not be so much an offer to buy as a desire to purchase space within the bookstore."

"Ah." Rio leaned forward and nodded. "This explains the reaction of the previous bookstore owner. I admit, since English is not my first language, I may not have put together a proposal that is as clear as I would like it to be. I had a Japanese-to-English translator prepare this set."

Ami bit the corner of her lower lip. Translations were a difficult thing in any industry. It was hard to verify the quality of a translation, and contract language was complicated. She could understand how the nuance might not have been presented clearly. "That's why we ask questions and discuss the details, right?"

"Yes." Rio did smile this time, a small smile, but a real one. "I appreciate your desire to clarify rather than refusing me outright."

Ami laughed but cringed inwardly. Hopefully she didn't sound too strained. Rio's interest in the bookstore had been the primary motive Mel had listed in their notes. Ami wondered if she was being too obvious asking about it. She decided to follow through, going over each of her notes with Rio to clarify the intent of the proposal.

While they discussed the bookstore, Lucien wandered around the area. He stayed in sight the entire time, his hands clasped behind his back. Rio glanced at him once in a while but made no comment. Once they'd reached the end of the document and Ami had thanked Rio, Lucien cleared his throat.

"Miss Matsumoto, you mentioned this fan is a family heirloom." He inclined his head to indicate something in another room off the living area, out of sight. "Could you tell me more about it and some of the other interesting items in here?"

Rio was at Lucien's side in a flash, leaving Ami to scramble out of her chair to join them. She almost tripped over an umbrella leaning against the leg of the table.

There was indeed a gorgeous feather fan sitting on a carved stand at the edge of a heavy executive office desk. The feathers of the fan were black and as glossy as Rio's hair, spread to form a graceful oval. They were bound at the base into a single handle wrapped in some kind of cord. Maybe silk?

"Yes." Rio stood and joined Lucien, who was standing in front of the fan. "It is one of the only family heirlooms I brought with me from Japan. I couldn't bear to be without it."

"I can understand that." Lucien paused, then lifted his hand in a signal for Ami to stop coming over. "It holds very old magic."

Ami looked from Lucien to the fan to Rio, then back again. There was tension building. Uncertain, she considered the far wall.

"These all look . . . very well maintained." Ami kept her hands clasped behind her back as she admired the collection of sharp-edged objects displayed on the wall.

She wasn't sure they were all daggers. They ranged from the length of a finger to the length of her entire forearm. They all caught the light as she moved to study them from different angles, and they all looked exceedingly sharp.

"Ah, well." Rio laughed and it came out as a sharp caaaaa. "I appreciate balance and elegance. I like variety in what I use to open my letters and packages."

Ami swallowed. Some of the documents Mel had reviewed with her and Lucien this morning had included more detail on what happened to Nancy. The previous bookstore owner hadn't drowned and washed up on the shore. She'd been slashed and sliced up by something. It hadn't been bites or claws. Something with a straight edge had cut into her flesh multiple times, and Nancy had bled out into the seawater of the Puget Sound. Ami's stomach twisted as she continued to look at the collection of blades.

Lucien joined her and leaned close to each weapon.

"None of those has tasted blood here on this island, wolf." Rio's voice had gone a few notes deeper, and she emitted a nasal growl. "I have gone out of my way to offer no threat, no insult. Yet here you are, sniffing around for blood like a scavenger."

They stared at each other. Ami realized it would be a bad thing to be caught between them as Lucien turned his body slightly to keep her behind him. She glanced around to determine what routes she had to get out of the room and out of the house.

"I have offered my hospitality, here, and I have no intention to hurt her. You, wolf, would be able to smell if I lied." Rio was still speaking to Lucien, but Ami was her obvious focus.

That brought a weird mix of anxiety and relief.

Lucien remained tense for another long moment, then he relaxed a fraction and sighed. "If your intentions are peaceful, why don't you pour more tea and we can discuss what it means to be a supernatural joining the community here in Wolfsound."

SEVEN

L ucien's control was the best in the pack. It was part of what qualified him as the next in line to lead. And yet, being around Amihan had tested him. She was annoying most of the time, even infuriating in certain moments.

What was with her ability to give truly epic side-eye, anyway? And the way she could shut down and make it absolutely clear she had no use for him at all. He had better things to do with his time than worry about her opinion of him.

He fumed as they walked back to the bookstore. He'd told her he would be her escort as they checked out Matsumoto Rio, and he'd kept his word. He hadn't expected the woman to be a supernatural. The overwhelming need to protect Amihan in that household had caught him by surprise.

Worse, Matsumoto Rio had been able to completely hide her nature until he'd found the fan. It had been old and full of power.

His stomach twisted uncomfortably. Amihan had been

seated at the woman's table, sipping tea with an unknown —someone who had come into town hiding what they were. Amihan was so human, so vulnerable. He would've never let her step into that house if he had been aware. He'd almost given himself over to the beast aspect of himself in his anger, his immediate need to get Amihan out of there before history could repeat itself.

"I'm sorry." Amihan's voice was quiet, and a little breathless.

Lucien halted suddenly, realizing he'd been walking too fast. He had his hand on Amihan's elbow forcing her to keep pace with him. Guilt burned in his gut, but he couldn't quite bring himself to release her. He loosened his hold though, until his fingers were only a light touch around her arm.

"You didn't do anything wrong," he answered. There was a lot of wolf in his voice, rough and an octave lower than usual.

She hadn't. Not really. She'd done exactly as she'd said she would. If anything, it had been her warm and engaging personality that had opened the door for them to step inside Matsumoto Rio's lair and learn as much as they had. He doubted Matsumoto Rio would have had so much restraint if it hadn't been for Amihan, and he knew for a fact he wouldn't have.

"You're angry though, and I made things harder for you in there." Amihan's teeth caught at her lower lip. "You would have been in a better position to deal with Rio if you hadn't had to worry about me."

He wanted to lean in close and kiss away the small hurt she had given her lip. This was the majority of his control problem, right here.

He cleared his throat and forced himself to gaze into her

deep umber eyes. "True. But it was because of your presence that we both held back, and that gave us the chance to talk."

"It could have gone badly, though, couldn't it? She said she didn't mean me any harm, but she didn't say whether she killed Nancy or not. I don't know what a tengu can do, but you said the fan contained very old magic. I remember something about tengu carrying people away in old folklore. I'd have to look them up, but I remember reading—"

"Amihan." He cut her off, mostly because he didn't want her to spiral further in her line of thought.

She was tense and worried, and it would be bad for the both of them if her fear became more than the hint he could smell in her scent right now. His need to protect her was already riding him, and anyone else coming along could tip him over the edge. He would end up lashing out, even harming whoever that might be.

He could claim it was too close to the full moon, but he wasn't about to give himself the excuse. The way he had managed to keep the people around him safe over the years, and to prevent the exposure of werewolves to human scrutiny, was to know when he did and did not have himself under control.

"Let me walk you home." He could do that. It was the best course of action. He could ensure her safety and then leave her with the bookstore and go for a run to clear his head.

She studied him, her gaze going straight through him, and he held very still. Waiting for what she would see of him.

"You're dangerous." She didn't sound afraid as she made the statement. It was more like she was searching with her words and her gaze. "Aren't you?"

"Yes." He wasn't going to lie or hide from her. In fact, he let a little of his wildness off leash and grinned at her, baring his teeth. He was proud of what he was. "The tengu is old. Older than me and so she has had time to gather power. But I could have ripped her to pieces before she got her hand on that fan of hers. She shouldn't have faced me without it. I bet you she won't from here on out."

He watched Amihan absorb his statements and calmed as he saw the acceptance in her expression and posture. He added, "I would not have let her carry you away."

Some of the tension eased from her shoulders, and color came back into her complexion. Her heart rate was still up, but fear was fading from her scent.

Amihan swallowed. "Am I stupid for not being afraid of you?"

A piece of something settled into place inside him. She knew what he was, was actively trying to learn what that meant. Her acceptance of him brought on a calm and a hunger he didn't want to bury under irritation anymore.

"Yes." He let his desire slip the leash even more and stepped farther into her space. "But I won't hurt you."

She didn't back away. He shifted his touch from her elbow to her shoulder, keeping it light, giving her a way out. He should tell her that the way she was looking up at him was a challenge. He should warn her to put distance between them before the expectation of something more developed between them.

Or he could tempt her to stay near him. He brought up his other hand and brushed her jaw with a fingertip.

"There's a lot I need to learn about the people here," she whispered, her eyes flitting from his gaze to his mouth and back again.

Heat pooled low in his belly and he chuckled. "Yes."

If she wasn't going to run from this, he wasn't going to hold her at arm's length anymore. Everything he'd done from childhood to the adult he was now had been out of responsibility to his pack's survival. Amihan's return to the island had made him feel alive.

Recognition allowed him to embrace how he felt, and the constant feeling of being off balance vanished. Now, he was a man with a new mission.

"There's a lot you need to remember too." He slid his hand up her jaw and into her soft hair until he was cradling her head by the nape of her neck. "You used to live here. Your family didn't know about the community here, but you've always been observant. Your intuition has always been strong. And when we were kids, you weren't afraid of me back then either."

"What were we to each other back then?" she asked, her voice breathless. Her scent had warmed with arousal, adding a slight tang to the sweet earthiness he'd recognized as hers.

"Kids." That's all they'd been. "Competitors in school. You were always reading, always studying. We both had our own things to prove and we traded top honors in classes every week, every test. You were the only one in class worth my time."

She'd irritated the hell out of him back then too. Because she hadn't been afraid of him. She'd been so smart, some thought too smart. He might have been one of a few real dangers in that school, but there had been bullies among both the supernaturals and the humans. Because she'd been his rival, he'd underestimated how fragile her humanity made her.

Guilt and shame and regret snuck up on him, the sour taste of them spreading across his tongue. "You need to remember what happened back then so you can decide if you want to trust me now."

Confusion clouded her eyes, and her brows drew together in consternation. She stiffened in his hands.

Ruefully, he let her go, his hands dropping to his sides. He didn't want what was in their history to come up later. He'd rather she make her decisions based on it all, and if he had to swim the Puget Sound to bring that damned muse back here to remove whatever block he'd placed on Amihan to keep thoughts of their childhood from occurring to her, Lucien would.

But knowing the muse, this wasn't a spell to be broken. Those wore off with time. It was a suggestion, a rerouting of a path in the mind so thoughts didn't wander in that direction. Forging new pathways took conscious effort.

"You could tell me, but that would be too easy, wouldn't it?" she muttered. "This is payback for how pissed you were with me earlier today, isn't it?"

"No, this isn't payback." He ground his teeth. It was the right thing to do.

He wanted to howl his frustration. Because, damn it, he wanted her. Fine. He could admit it inside his own mind.

And she wanted him. It was clear in her scent and the way she let him touch her. They were standing here on the side of the road where anyone could come across them, and he wanted nothing more than to invite her for a romp in the woods.

It would be wrong. Irresponsible. A risk for her. Because she didn't know everything she needed to make an informed decision.

He sighed. "Let me walk you home."

They walked back in silence, and he could almost hear the gears turning in her head the whole way. His dark mood lightened. He couldn't stay angry, not even at his past self, when he was near her. That alone made it worth torturing himself with her proximity. He had always liked the way her brain never stopped. He wanted to know more about the adult she'd become.

~

Wow.

Ami stood on the back patio of the bookstore watching Taffy check the perimeter of the small patch of backyard before doing his business in his designated corner. She was still replaying every moment of the walk back to the bookstore with Lucien.

Her cheeks were still flushed, and the fluttering in her chest kept intensifying until she had to consciously breathe through it all. This was what a squee felt like in real life. She was all exclamation points and giddy emojis. She was a walking interrobang when it came to Lucien.

Moving around helped her disperse some of the nervous energy bubbling up from her center as she thought about how close he'd been, about the way the lightest touch from him set her nerves firing off in tingling waves of excitement. She wanted more.

When she'd first arrived, she'd been determined to build a solid foundation for the next phase of her life without any distractions. Scratch that. She'd always been too cautious in her previous dating experiences, trying to keep her head and preserve her heart. Why not change these old habits too and dive in this time? It could backfire painfully, but it might be worth the risk. It felt like it'd be worth it.

Taffy trotted to her, and the two of them went back

inside the bookstore. Lights turned on as they entered. She'd noticed the lights going on and off on their own as she moved from one floor to another. The first night, she'd thought it was motion sensors and vowed to find the master switch. Now, she wondered.

"Thank you," she whispered to the bookstore as she climbed the stairs to the upper living area and the lights came on ahead of her.

It might have been her imagination, but the wood of the banister under her hand warmed slightly too.

This was a mystic bookstore. The talking tortoise said so.

So had Lucien. He'd also been clear that he didn't know much of anything else about how the bookstore worked. Taffy probably knew, having belonged here before she had. He was a cheerful dog most of the time, but at times when he was lying flat on his belly with his head on his front paws, she thought she caught a sad look in his eyes. She might be projecting onto Taffy, but she thought he was the type of heart to want to make her feel welcome even when he was mourning his previous companion. It was safe to guess Taffy was tied into the magic of the bookstore as well.

When she reached the landing of the upper living area, she bent to unlace her boots. There might be space for a small combination bench and shoe rack here. It'd be nice to have a spot to sit and take off the combat boot–style shoes she liked for casual days. She'd need at least a small shoe rack to keep her shoes neatly stored but convenient for when she wanted to head downstairs into a more public space or outside.

She paused in her pondering and looked at her corgi companion. "Taffy, do you talk?"

Taffy gave her a sharp, happy-sounding bark. Then he sat and panted, looking pleased with himself.

"I mean, do you talk to people, the way Genbu does?" She was convinced Taffy understood her. But then, most dogs had a lot more cognitive skills than people generally gave them credit for.

Taffy tipped his head to one side, whined a little, and gave her a soft woof. His big brown eyes looked eager to please.

"I'm going to take that as a no." She bent to cup his face in her hands, and her fingers massaged the base of his ears. "That's okay, I like you this way. We can understand each other just fine."

Taffy dropped his jaw in a doggie grin and gave her cheek a quick lick. Ami laughed and stood up. Two more steps and she was basically in the kitchen area, which had a tiny breakfast nook looking out over the harbor. There was a window seat there, just the right size for her to sit and read if she wanted. Or she could enjoy a meal for one at the table right next to it. It felt perfect to her.

"I'll get dinner started for me, then we'll get you yours."

Her rice cooker was one of two electronics she'd brought with her in her huge duffel bag. She'd set it up the first night she'd arrived and picked up rice as part of her grocery run for basics.

"It won't take long."

Trey and Lucien had helped her, taking her first to the town grocery for general staples, then to Det's Thai restaurant, which had a small Asian market attached, for other basics she needed for her day-to-day. So there was already warm, fragrant jasmine rice waiting for her.

She'd figured her day was going to be busy, so she'd set chicken thighs to marinate that morning in a marinade of soy sauce and generous amounts of freshly crushed garlic cloves. She took the marinade container out of the refrigerator, gave the contents a quick stir, and set it on the counter next to the stove.

"I'm really glad Det has that little Asian mart so I don't have to order and ship stuff I need. I bet Rio will be happy too." She'd said it out loud, sort of talking to herself. But Taffy gave her a quiet woof and she thought it sounded like agreement.

There was one big pot she could use for stew, and it was too hard to cook for one, so she always cooked enough to have leftovers for a few meals later. It would save her time around lunch once she actually got into a routine running the bookstore.

"I bet Rio has really nice kitchen knives, since she's got the gorgeous collection of blades in her study. Seems like she'd know how to take care of them." Images of the police reports flashed in Ami's mind, in particular, the notes on the way Nancy had died. She'd been sliced up.

"That was probably why Lucien got all worked up," Ami muttered, unsettled. Her initial reaction was to want to be friends with Rio, but that whole wall of sharp-edged weapons was hard to set aside.

She drizzled oil into the pot and set the burner under it to high. There weren't any tongs, so Ami made do with the plastic spatula, promising herself a trip back to one of the stores on her street for some cooking utensils. Speaking of kitchen knives, the ones here were very basic. Nancy didn't seem to have cooked a whole lot. Ami wondered, idly, if Lucien cooked. Ever. He was a werewolf, after all.

"I wonder if he prefers his meals . . . fresh." Ami considered that.

The oil was almost smoking hot, so she added in the

chicken thighs, careful to avoid the splatter of hot oil. While they were browning, she pulled out some bay leaves and white peppercorns. After a couple of minutes of turning the thighs so they browned evenly, she added the marinade liquid right into the pot, then the seasonings.

"He ate at Det's restaurant, and he can take spicy food." Better than her, actually.

She grabbed the glass measuring cup she kept under her water boiler, measured out some readily hot water, and poured it into the marinade container. She gave the container a swish to get what was left of the marinade, then poured the water into the pot too.

Her water boiler was the other kitchen gadget she'd brought with her. As far as she knew, it wasn't a common US kitchen appliance, but her parents' household always had one as she was growing up. She liked having one of her own.

"Mel said Lucien went to university in the UK, but he drank coffee this morning. I wonder if he likes tea?"

Her boiler wasn't a teakettle or a hot water pot. It sat on the counter and held a reservoir of water, bringing it to a boil and maintaining it at her selected temperature around the clock. She had almost-boiling water available to her at the push of a button for cooking, for tea, or for whatever. That and the rice cooker made a kitchen home for her.

"I wonder if werewolves eat rice."

Nothing about the building around her moved, but she got the distinct impression both the dog and the . . . room were listening.

"Well, I know dogs can eat rice," she said to Taffy, and the room. "But we won't give you rice to try unless you have some kind of gastrointestinal indiscretion. It's more of a settle-an-upset-tummy sort of thing for you, I think. I'll have to do some research on it and check the ingredients in your dog food."

Taffy lifted his head and gave her a doggie grin.

She set the burner to medium-low and placed a lid on the pot so it was partially, but not completely, covered. "I'll just leave this to simmer for a while."

She shoved her feet back into her boots at the landing, not bothering to lace them since she only intended to stay inside, and started down the stairs again. The lights turned on ahead of her.

She smiled. This was kind of nice, like she wasn't alone. "Thank you."

Taffy followed her as she grabbed her traveler's notebook and favorite fountain pen from behind the register and went all the way down to the basement level reader's room. Mel had taken their files back to the station with them, but the sticky notes were still on the wall. Ami briefly wondered whether she should have taken a picture of the wall, then taken them down. Sure, they'd locked the door to the reading room when they'd left, but it had opened readily when she'd returned just now.

Unless it was the bookstore. She realized no door in the bookstore was ever locked when she actually needed to go through it. Doors were locked when she did a check of them all before going to bed, but never when she was just moving around from room to room. The first day, Helen had said the front door to the bookstore was locked, but it had opened for Ami. She wondered if that was a part of the magic of the bookstore.

She looked up at the ceiling. "You're subtle, aren't you?"

The lights in the reading room dimmed slightly then came back to full brightness. All right then. Talking out loud to the building was not just for her benefit. Good to know.

She looked at the board and the three individuals she'd identified as their top people of interest to rule out. Trey had a provable alibi, even if he had been alone. Mel would confirm his streaming log in. Yay, Asian dramas.

Matsumoto Rio was a more complicated situation. The reason she had been under suspicion had been because everyone thought she'd wanted to buy the bookstore, which wasn't the case. In fact, it seemed that Rio clearly understood she couldn't just buy it. Ami wasn't sure how property and deeds and legal considerations worked in the human world, but it was clear something about the bookstore's magic ensured the store went to the person of its choosing.

She'd have to ask Mel or maybe one of the elder townspeople what happened when someone bought the property that was not chosen by the bookstore itself.

Recent memories popped into her mind. Lights going on and off themselves. Doors locking and unlocking on their own. An image of the front door hitting Lucien in the ass on his way out that first night. She giggled. Okay, there were plenty of people who would be too spooked to stay. She hadn't connected all those coincidences until just now, but all in all, it was enough to make a person wonder if a place was at least haunted.

Rio wouldn't have wanted a haunted place that didn't want her, would she? Still, all those blades on the wall weren't something to ignore. Rio had been very defensive about them too. Amihan wasn't sure how much of that had been a response to the possibility of them suspecting her for Nancy's murder and how much had been Rio reacting to Lucien.

The third person on the wall was one who Ami hadn't thought to talk to. Technically, he had an alibi. He had been at the police station, arrested for drunk and disorderly conduct. But he had gotten into a fight with Nancy earlier that day and he would, theoretically, know who else was in Nancy's life. Wouldn't he? So even if he had an alibi, maybe he could provide a lead to one of the other suspects.

Really, someone needed to talk to him. Tomorrow. Ami made a mental note to mention it, but it was just as likely Mel already had it planned. Or Lucien might pay him a visit tonight. She'd find out tomorrow.

For the time being, she moved the sticky note for Trey to one side, in an area she'd mentally decided was clear for now. If new information came up, it would put him back into consideration. There was still the question of all those blades in Rio's home. Honestly though, she liked him and Rio both. She hoped they both came through in the clear.

Her updates complete, she left the reading room, locking the door behind her. Then she headed up to the main floor to do her nightly check of all the doors and windows. She paused at the front door, catching a glimpse of something red.

Huh. Someone had left an umbrella leaning in the entryway outside the front door. She started to reach for the door handle, then thought better of it. Whoever it was might come back to get it—best to leave it out there. She might get some curtains for the windows and front door though. It was a little creepy to have all those open windows for anyone to look in, especially in the dark, even if this was a bookstore.

By the time she got all the way back up to the kitchen, she was a little out of breath. All the stairs would be good to keep her in shape. Whew.

The kitchen was filled with the rich umami smell of her adobo. She lifted the cover off the pot and added a few splashes of white vinegar. After giving it a stir, she tasted it, then added just a little sugar too, to deepen the flavor. She let it continue to simmer while she popped open the top of the rice cooker and scooped a helping of steaming-hot jasmine rice into a bowl. Finally, she spooned the chicken adobo over her rice.

Simple dinner for one, with plenty left over for a couple of future meals. Done.

She sat in the window seat, holding the bowl in her hands and eating with just a spoon. Her parents would have wanted her to sit at the table and use a spoon and fork, but honestly, it was just her and Taffy. Taffy would get his dinner after she finished hers, and he would not be getting people food. As she looked out on the harbor, she thought about what Lucien had said to her again.

"He wants me to remember, but what? Him? Something he said or did? Something I said or did?"

Funny thing was, she honestly didn't remember him. She didn't remember anyone she'd gone to school with when she'd lived here on the island. But cooking, like she had tonight, she remembered a kitchen. She remembered helping her mother cook and her father preparing dinner on some nights.

She remembered sitting on the floor at a low coffee table with the rice cooker at one end, in a living room, enjoying dinner with her parents in front of the one TV in the house. It wasn't that they had no dining room table. They'd just eaten at the coffee table while watching television as casual family time. She hadn't thought about those day-to-day memories in forever. Maybe it just took some associated activities to help her remember.

And she wanted to remember Lucien, if only to understand his incredibly frustrating insistence that she should. Because at this moment, she wasn't sure if she wanted to grab him by the front of his shirt and shake straight answers out of him or to rip off his shirt and kiss him.

She was pretty certain he would have let her kiss him.

As she cleaned up her dishes and put away her food, she wondered if she should make time the next day to wander over to the elementary and middle schools. They were within walking distance.

She wondered if she would remember. If she'd want to.

CHAPTER
EIGHT

L ucien scowled as he and Mel crossed the school playing fields. School had been out for hours and even the after-school sports activities were wrapping up. Wolfsound was a small town, and the sports fields were used by grades K-12. Because they were shared, the town could focus on ensuring the facilities were at least kept in good condition. For Lucien, the history here was filled with lessons learned and guilt.

"You're going to make small children cry if you keep that expression on your face." Mel nudged him with their elbow.

He shot them a sideways glance, then did what he could to smooth out his expression.

Mel choked back a laugh. "I take it back. Brooding expression and burning look of death if anyone dares to cross your path is still better than your blank look, where I don't know what you're thinking and whether you might just decide to destroy everything around you at any moment. Go back to being annoyed at the world."

Lucien lifted his upper lip and snarled at them, but the heavy mood he'd been carrying dissipated somewhat.

Mel smiled and lifted their coffee cup in salute. "That's an improvement. Would you be in a better mood if we'd stopped by to debrief at a certain bookstore owner on Main Street?"

An image of Amihan popped into his mind, her face open with curiosity and a touch of suspicion whenever she realized it was him. He almost smiled before he caught himself. Even if he was irritated with Mel for bringing Amihan up in conversation, he couldn't say he didn't welcome thinking of her.

"Maybe," he admitted.

Mel spit their coffee.

He didn't bother to hide his half smile. He wasn't a pup going through his first crush. There was no reason to hide his interest in a person, once that person was aware. He was reasonably sure he'd been clear to Amihan yesterday. What was torturing him now was his own decision to give her some space to think about it. Instead of spending more time with her, he'd gone in wolf form to the third suspect's home and sniffed around the property, if only to rule out a potential threat to the town, his pack, and Amihan.

"In more professional topics," he drawled, deciding to redirect Mel's midafternoon caffeinated energy. "Are you planning to invite Nancy's ex back to the police station?"

Mel shook their head. "Just a few questions for Declan Simpa, while you take some deep breaths around his truck. He should be here working his coaching job."

"Huh," Lucien mused. "I thought he ran the cutter that picks up tourists from Seattle to give them tours."

"It's off-season."

"Ah. So this is his second job." Several people on the island had seasonal work.

Mel nodded. "Did you find anything at his house?"

"Other than a disturbing mountain of unwashed socks, no." Lucien wrinkled his nose. "Nothing suspicious around his house or backyard and no obvious tools for arson or murder. There was a second-story window open, so I was able to slip in and take a sniff around inside too. It's a bachelor pad, for sure, and he isn't the type of person to keep up with his laundry or dishes. Other than that, no signs of egregious behavior."

He paused—something had been bothering him since his morning scouting trip.

"Huh." Mel sipped at their coffee thoughtfully. "I mean, the man has an alibi. This just further confirms he didn't commit either crime."

Lucien would have responded, but a whistle blew, drawing their attention to a line of kids jogging around the corner of one of the school buildings. The person they'd come to see, Declan Simpa, was riding a golf cart alongside them. Lucien snorted. Declan Simpa was an able-bodied man who prided himself on his physical prowess. He had photos on his walls of his numerous mud runs and obstacle course–type achievements. It seemed odd that Simpa wouldn't run alongside the students he spent his time coaching. Then again, Simpa did a lot of talking about what others should do or think and didn't appear to take his own advice.

Mel was in uniform and immediately caught the attention of the kids and their person of interest. The kids gave Mel a friendly wave and a few polite, out of breath greetings.

Declan brought the cart to a stop and blew his whistle

again. "All right. Good conditioning workout. We're done for the day."

The children dispersed. Declan stepped out of the cart and stood, his arms crossed over his chest in a defensive stance. When a few of the kids lingered, he glared at them until they took themselves off the fields. Lucien supposed he couldn't blame the man. The kids were certain to run home to their parents with news that the town sheriff had paid their coach a visit today. It was bound to give rise to some questions.

Lucien might feel some concern for Declan Simpa, but the man was no saint.

"Harassing a man at his place of work isn't ethical, Sheriff." Declan spat to one side sneering at Mel.

Lucien stiffened at the implication and the lack of respect, but he waited. This man was a piece of work, but nothing Mel couldn't handle.

"Had some questions for you," Mel responded, unbothered. "Seeing as you depend on tourists for your primary source of income, I thought I'd come here, so we keep everything just among us town folk."

"You asked plenty of questions before. Are you just looking for an excuse to pin more charges on me? I notice you haven't found the killer yet." The breeze carried Declan's scent to Lucien.

The man smelled of salty sea from the sound, rust and oil from his boat, and stale sweat from his rumpled polo and cargo pants. He appeared reasonably put together—none of his clothing was brand new and nothing was overly worn or in need of replacing. Parents trusted him to coach their kids because he was an average man; they probably considered him dependable. Salt of the earth and all that. Maybe that was why Nancy had liked him.

"You were drunk, Declan." Mel made the statement matter-of-factly.

"No law against having a few drinks," Declan grumbled. "I was taking a walk to clear my head."

"You were stumbling around shouting, kicking trash cans into buildings, and throwing stuff into the street." Mel clarified. "Being drunk in public is not a crime in the state of Washington, but we can still arrest an intoxicated person for disorderly conduct. This is a small town and people who live here year-round appreciate the quiet. It was best to bring you in and let you sleep it off."

"Who's to say I wasn't on my way home? I make a few rude comments and you haul me in for the night."

Mel didn't say more, and Lucien remained silent. This wasn't what they'd come to discuss with Declan. The man obviously had simmering anger and resentment though. It could be his way of mourning the loss of his ex. Or it could be something else.

"You were dating Nancy for quite some time." Mel took out their phone and consulted their notes.

"We were exclusive for months," Declan shot back.

"Was she spending time with anyone else?"

"There was that Trey person." It sounded like Trey's name was an unpleasant kind of sour in Declan's mouth. "Always hanging around the bookstore. He's out at night all the time and I don't see you hauling him in for it. A couple of the other bookstore regulars were around who didn't always buy books."

Mel dutifully noted the handful of names. "Did Nancy meet with any of these people outside the bookstore? Did she meet with anyone else outside the bookstore?"

Declan shook his head. "I mean, Nancy went out and about on errands and stuff. Talked to people along the way.

But she didn't meet up with anyone specifically to hang out. She hated coming with me to the bar for trivia night. Said it was too many people, too noisy."

While Mel continued to ask questions and Declan responded, Lucien stepped away and wandered around the cart. He also walked to the nearby parking lot and back again. Nothing unexpected. No incriminating scents. He was almost disappointed. There was something about Declan, the way he glared at everyone and the way he almost challenged them to find something to hold against him. Lucien's gut told him there was something hidden.

As Lucien returned to where Mel and Declan were standing, their conversation reached his ears.

Mel seemed to be wrapping up a review of Declan's official statement. ". . . but you were at the police station that night."

"Yes, I have an alibi," Declan said quickly. "As you know."

Mel cleared their throat. "You also had a public fight with the victim during the day before you went on a drunken bender later that evening, cursing her, the bookstore, and everything she owned, Declan."

"But it wasn't my fault," Declan protested, waving his arms to make his point. "Nancy made me do it, the way she was overreacting earlier that day. We were perfect together, she knew that. I only asked her to stop spending so much time with other people, wasting so much effort in that stupid bookstore. She was just too sensitive, no wonder no one really liked her."

Mel scowled.

Declan shook his head. "At this point though, I don't want to speak ill of the dead. I just want to focus on the good."

Everyone mourned in different ways, but Lucien thought Declan didn't seem to be all that broken up about Nancy's demise.

"Well, thank you for your time, Declan." Mel sighed. "Investigation is ongoing and I may come back with more questions. Same thing as I said before, don't leave town, please."

"Fine, fine," Declan grumbled. "This better be wrapped up before the tourist season kicks in. You could be hurting my business if I can't make my trips."

"We'll talk about it when the time comes." There was a hard edge to Mel's tone now.

Lucien smirked. Mel didn't give much slack to people who played the victim and made a situation all about themselves. That was what irritated Lucien about Declan. So far, it'd been all about him and how the events had impacted him. There'd been no concern or real feelings expressed about the loss of Nancy.

He fell in beside Mel as they walked away. After a distance, they spoke quietly, for his ears only. "Something is off. The timing is too suspicious for him not to have had something to do with the fire at the bookstore at least."

"Agreed. But no incriminating scents on his vehicle. No accelerants aside from the fuel in his gas tank. Nancy's scent is in the passenger seat, but that doesn't implicate him since they dated. No blood." Movement off to one side drew Lucien's attention.

"Good to know. I'm glad you have the same suspicions as I do, but I need proof." Mel muttered a curse. "I'm going to head back to the police station to check in."

Taffy was romping around, jumping on and off the back of Genbu's huge tortoise shell as Genbu made his way across the fields. Suddenly, Taffy stopped. Both the corgi and the tortoise stretched their necks and swiveled their heads to watch Declan get in his truck and drive away.

Taffy wouldn't be out and about away from the bookstore unless . . .

Lucien looked out over the fields and bleachers and caught sight of someone.

"All right. If you don't need my nose anymore, I'm going to go on about my business." Lucien kept his gaze on a lone figure sitting on the bleachers. The wind was blowing in the wrong direction for her scent to go to him, but he knew the wind carried sweet plumeria intertwined with earthy ylang ylang.

Mel paused, then chuckled. "Your business. Gotcha. Text me when it's a good time to head back to the bookstore to go over information again. I want another look at the mind map she created."

Lucien nodded.

Mel walked away toward the front of the schools. Lucien headed for the bleachers, where Amihan was sitting.

NINE

A mihan saw Lucien coming. Or at least, a part of her registered his approach. She felt strangely detached, like she was an outsider watching a combination of scenes from now and brief flashes of some other time.

She hadn't had a good reason to go inside either the elementary or middle school and hadn't wanted to bother any school faculty or staff for permission to roam the hallways. Meandering around the outside, mostly the playground and sports fields, had been enough.

She heard the sounds of laughter—of children laughing at her, not with her. She heard whispers about her, not to her. Teachers had spoken over her head to each other, or to her parents. No one had been cruel, not openly so. But the callous comments and criticisms had been cumulative, and Ami remembered now why she only felt comfortable in the school library or at the bookstore. Those had been the peaceful places in her early life.

Sitting on the bleachers had been another thing she

used to do. But this didn't bring her peace. She'd been here for a while, sitting in the discomfort, nudging at it the way she would worry at a sore tooth.

Lucien joined her without a word, sitting close enough for her to feel the heat of his presence against her shoulder without him touching her. The stiff breeze coming up from the harbor didn't have as much bite while he was close.

"We went to school here." She didn't know why she said it, only that it was what came to mind when she decided she didn't want silence between them.

"Yes." His tone was easygoing. After a moment, he added, "You're still the first student to have checked out and read every book in the school library."

She huffed out a laugh. "I'm sure there've been other students over the years who've managed to do it too."

He shrugged and leaned forward to rest his elbows on his knees. "New books come in and old books get retired, but you were the first to do it and you could prove to the librarian you actually read every one of the books. Even if another student has been inspired to repeat the feat, you did it first."

"Ha." She smiled, finally. "I might have a completionist streak."

One corner of his mouth pulled back in a lopsided grin. "You think?"

She looked out over the fields, at the fences around the baseball diamond and the other areas for other sports. There wasn't a lot, but there was something for almost everyone. Her gaze fell to her feet, past the bleachers, and through the gaps in the seating to the ground below. No one was there.

"There were bullies at this school," she whispered. "But I guess every school has them. Or the potential for them."

"Yes." His response was the same as before in a lot of ways. Same word, same length of time it took to utter the one syllable. But his tone had dropped a few notes deeper, and there was an edge that hadn't been there before.

"I didn't have a lot of friends." She didn't have as much conviction in that statement. It was more like she didn't want it to be true. "I don't remember any, actually. But I think if I had them, I would have tried to keep in touch somehow. Letters, back when we were kids. Long-distance phone calls would have been expensive though. Maybe keeping in touch wasn't all that practical."

The world had been different twenty years ago. She remembered still using pay phones to call her parents to pick her up after school, if she didn't just walk home by herself.

"No, you didn't have a lot of friends," Lucien confirmed.

She smiled but didn't particularly feel any happiness in the smile. She didn't want to lie to herself either. "I appreciate the honesty."

He didn't say anything further.

That was okay. She still had thoughts. She decided to give them voice, out loud. "But I liked to study, I loved tests. I remember studying at home or coming to the library, or going straight to the bookstore. And I remember here. I've been sitting here trying to figure out why I remember these bleachers."

"You sat here sometimes, out in the open where anyone could see you, in full sight of the teachers," Lucien answered her. "It had been a smart move. Teachers would notice if you moved from this spot. It was riskier to try to pull you under the bleachers when the teachers knew where to look for you."

She shuddered. She wasn't ready to think about that yet. They'd been young, only in middle school at most.

She wanted to remember more about him. "You didn't participate in sports, did you?"

He snorted. "No."

She raised an eyebrow, figuring he could see her expression out of the corner of his eye even if he wasn't looking straight at her. "You seem pretty strong."

He was looming next to her, literally sheltering her from the breeze. She thought she had a memory of a much-younger version of him. His boyish features sharper, his arms and legs too long for his body, and his hands and feet slightly too big. He'd been gawkier back then, and it would be years before he grew into the sculpted and mature man he was now. In profile, she found him to be very handsome. Maybe because he wasn't smirking at her.

No. She'd be lying to herself if she tried to convince herself she didn't like his smirk. It infuriated her, but it also stirred up all sorts of fluttering low in her belly.

"I was too strong," he said, his voice still quiet. "I was forbidden to play in sports with the human kids. I didn't have the control yet to blend and stay undiscovered."

Right. Werewolf.

She nodded. "That makes sense."

She needed to learn more about the supernatural elements of the town.

"You didn't seem to like the team sports either." He turned to look at her, his gaze searching.

She guessed he was trying to gauge how much she remembered.

She shook her head. "My high school had a swim team. I liked it because I didn't really have to talk with my teammates. I just got to swim. I'm guessing they didn't have one here."

"No." His expression was so carefully neutral. Unreadable.

"I don't remember whatever it is you want me to remember." She wanted to get that out there.

"Yes you do." He sat up straighter.

She pressed her lips together, annoyed. "Is it that important?"

He was such a jerk. But she was as irritated with herself for letting him get to her as she was with him for his attitude.

"I learned a lesson that day." His gaze continued to hold her as he spoke. "I think it's important that you remember so you can decide if you want to trust me now. I learned and I won't let it happen again."

She drew her brows together, thinking hard, intending to ask him what he meant, but then an image of the space beneath the bleachers came to her mind. She wanted to look, though she was nervous, but couldn't because his gaze still held hers. "You never played sports, but you were here too. You studied out here on the bleachers."

He nodded.

It was coming back to her.

"I was going to go to the bookstore and I fell." She closed her eyes. "Someone grabbed my ankle through the bleachers and yanked. I fell and it hurt so bad I screamed."

Images flashed and she remembered the antiseptic smell of a hospital. There'd been the sound of a helicopter too. She'd been flown out to a hospital on the mainland because of the compound fracture in her leg. She'd required surgery. She'd seen the documents in the file of medical history documents her mother kept for her.

He nodded. "We'd all taken the High School Placement Test. I was mad because you scored ahead of me, but I figured if I studied harder, I'd beat you in the PSATs. Others, though, they were mad at you. Embarrassed you scored well when they thought you didn't deserve to."

Yes. The top scores had been announced in class. People knew, and instead of being proud or excited to tell her parents, she'd been . . . afraid. "I wanted to go to the nurse's office or go home early, but I wasn't sick. It was better to be out here than in the cafeteria for lunch."

He nodded next to her. "It wasn't enough, not that time."

Hisses and whispered curses. Paper crumpled into tight balls, thrown at her in class. She'd wanted to get out of the building, get away until everyone had a chance to cool down and get distracted by something else.

"There were some kids who wouldn't let it go," she whispered.

"Yes." There was pain in Lucien's voice. "A handful of them came here, snuck under the bleachers. I knew they were lurking there beneath you, sneaking up on you. It would have taken speed and strength to get you away from them, or more to deal with them out of sight. I made a choice. I knew it was coming and I didn't help you."

A sound squeezed its way out of her chest and up through her throat. It was small and frightened, like a whimper, only worse because it was so quiet. She saw hands reach up through the bleachers, caught glimpses of nasty smiles. They had reached up and grabbed her ankles, yanked her down through the bleachers until pain had shot through her lower legs and made her scream.

"You ran for the teachers."

She had looked up through her tears and seen him sprinting across the field.

"Only as fast as a human could run." His voice was strained. "I had to keep hiding what I was. I didn't help you directly and I didn't get you help as fast as was possible."

Her heart squeezed as she heard the anguish in his voice. "That wasn't your fault."

"I could've seen it, heard it coming." The intensity in his tone made his voice shake just a little. "A wolf doesn't just hunt. We are aware of the other predators out there and we are supposed to be wily enough to avoid ambush by anything that would try to take us out. I had my sight and smell and hearing, but I hadn't used my brain to prevent it, head it off before it could happen."

She didn't want this for him. The child she was wouldn't have wanted him to punish himself this way. "You weren't responsible for me."

"I was." He stared at her, his eyes lightening to liquid quicksilver. "You were my rival. Mine. You were the only one who made school even a little interesting when I would rather have been out running the forests. You made human academics worth the effort. We had a competition, you and I. I shouldn't have let you get taken out by anyone else. Especially not that way."

He'd smirked as a child too. The image hung in her mind now. She remembered hating it then and loving the rush of seeing it wiped off his face when she did better in class, answered faster. She still had a love-hate relationship with his smirk.

"You were my rival too. None of the bullying in school mattered if I could keep competing with you." She reached out and placed her hand over his on the bleacher. "It wasn't you who hurt me."

His hand curled underneath hers into a fist. "But I didn't think or run fast enough, didn't use my head or abilities. I let you get seriously hurt. Your parents never let you come back to school. They moved as soon as they could get new jobs and sell their house. I made the wrong choice and you were gone."

AMIHAN PAUSED when Lucien came to a halt a few steps short of the bookstore. He'd walked her back from the schools, giving her silent space to process the maelstrom of thoughts spinning around in her mind. The walk helped her deal with the churning mess of feelings bubbling in her belly too. His presence had been comforting, reassuring, letting her know she had time before she had to respond to him. But here they were, at her door, and he looked as if he was going to leave.

She had to say something. Ask something. What did she want to know?

"What am I to you now?"

Ah no, they shouldn't start this out on the street. They should go inside. Maybe. He might not want to. Did she want him to?

His expression seemed calm, but his eyes were still a stormy grey. When he spoke, his words were so quiet, no one but her would have heard him even though they were outside. "You are still mine."

He hesitated, then added. "If you'll have me."

She should have been alarmed. From the first time he'd said *mine*, she had recognized she should pay attention to the signs. That kind of possessiveness should have been a

red flag. But something about the way he said it, the way he was looking at her, into her, went beyond certain words in the English language. It was more complicated than a word.

If you'll have me.

He was giving her a choice. It felt less about possession and more about choice—choosing to be his to . . . protect, maybe.

"By yours," she said slowly, watching him, "what do you mean?"

There was a stillness in his gaze, wild but hunter still. "Humans don't have a term for it. Exclusive comes close. This between us would only be you and me. And the commitment isn't just about intimacy. We protect and support each other. Nurture each other."

He'd been there since she'd arrived. Even when he hadn't intended to be there for her, he'd still helped her at every turn. He'd been thoughtful and considerate. He'd given her space too. He could have overwhelmed her, swept her off her feet, taken advantage of how new she was to the island and isolated her.

Instead, he'd facilitated her budding friendship with Trey. He'd given Mel room to hit on her, and then to become another new friend. Every moment he'd been around her had been a chance for him to be problematic, but he'd held back and given her room and now ensured she had all the knowledge he could think of to let her make an informed decision.

If he was asking her to be his, he was offering to be hers.

"Is there anything else you wanted me to know or wanted me to think about before I make a decision?" She should probably ask exactly what she was deciding. "Is this a point of no return? Some kind of lifetime-binding situation?"

He blinked. "No. I just . . ."

He fell silent, looking perplexed as he struggled for words.

"Needed to come clean?" she suggested.

"It sounds less earth-shattering now that it's all out in the open." He scratched the back of his head.

He'd walked back into her life full of confidence and a dash of arrogance, all smirk and infuriating self-assurance. As the big bad wolf, he was sexy as sin. Now, standing here, slightly embarrassed and off-balance, she found his expression incredibly endearing.

"It meant a lot to you," she whispered.

He'd wanted her to have the memory of all the history between them before she decided to tangle with him. He'd been right, too, because if she'd remembered after they'd gotten intimate, she would have been a jumble of emotions. She was a mess now, but it would have been worse, more confusing. It might have felt like a betrayal.

Instead, here and now, it felt like a promise.

She looked up at him, and she trusted him. More than she had before she'd remembered why she'd left this island, she trusted him. "It means a lot to me."

"Yeah?" He let his hand drop from the back of his head and moved forward a step or two.

The space between them had almost disappeared. Either one of them only had to lean in just a bit, and they would be touching. The air around them was warming, and she was so very aware of his physical proximity. If any part of them made contact with the other, there might be an actual spark.

"Yeah." She drank in the sight of this man. He cared so much about the people around him.

He'd been there to make sure Trey wouldn't get into trouble seeking out the bookstore again. Been there to give Mel support in their role as the sheriff of this town. Been there to help Ami feel safe. He would have ripped Rio apart for her sake. Her heart expanded in her chest until she thought she might burst.

He lifted his hand and brushed her jaw with gentle fingertips. Her skin tingled with his touch. Her chest tightened and she couldn't breathe; she was held by delicious anticipation. There was a wildness in his eyes, inviting her to come and play.

"All you have to do is tell me to stop, and I will." He was so close, his words whispered against her skin, and he was still giving her a way out.

She tilted her face up to him. "I'll tell you if I want you to stop."

He had wanted her to rebuild trust in him. He needed to trust her in turn. His fingertips traced a path from her jaw to her neck to the hollow behind her ear, until he cradled the nape of her neck in his palm. Her entire body was tingling, waiting for more.

"Do you want—"

She didn't let him finish; she leaned to close the space between them and crashed her lips into his in an impulsive kiss. Suddenly wanting him and no more words. Just him.

He tipped his head to meet her and fitted his mouth against hers. His arms hooked around her waist, then pulled her close as he made a quiet growling noise.

Oh. This was, yes, this was what she wanted. She melted against him at the sound and heard her own low moan in response.

His lips softened as he moved his mouth against hers, taking the lead in the kiss. When he parted his lips, his tongue flicked against the seam of her mouth, and she opened for him. As they deepened the kiss, tasting and learning each other, she closed her fists around the material of his shirt, wanting him closer. Lucien Allard was very good at kissing.

She arched her chest into him, and his hands moved over her, following the curve of her spine up her back, encouraging her to mold her body against his. He was so damned tall though, and she stumbled backward. He shot one hand out to brace them against the doorframe of the entrance to the bookstore, catching them both.

Happiness bubbled up inside her and she laughed. He grinned, pressing his forehead against hers.

"I want this," she whispered, breathless. Oh wow did she want this.

She took the moment to get air, her breaths ragged as she looked into his eyes. His eyes were dilated, his pupils blown wide and dark with an arousal she absolutely echoed. She reached behind her with one hand, fumbling until she found the doorknob and let them inside. The bookstore let them both in, no keys needed.

She gasped out a thank you to the building.

Lucien tipped his head to the side, a question forming in his expression. She only shook her head and slid her arms up and around his neck, pulling him back to her for another kiss. The pitter-patter of Taffy's claws against the wood floors announced his arrival as well.

Lucien bent his knees, then wrapped his arms around her thighs and lifted her as he straightened. Taffy let out an excited bark.

She squeaked, and heat burned her cheeks as embarrassment streaked through her. But he only chuckled and pressed a firm kiss against her mouth. "Where do you want to go?"

Oh. Right. There were a lot of windows here. Downstairs had a lot of book stacks and cozy corners, but also a reading room filled with the names of murder suspects.

"Upstairs," she whispered against his lips.

TEN

T he sun was rising earlier at this time of the year as days were getting longer. Lucien inhaled, enjoying the sweet floral scent of plumeria and earthy ylang ylang emanating from the very warm form curled against him. At the end of the bed, on Ami's side, Taffy stood, then dropped his front into a low dog stretch. She'd insisted on letting the corgi in as she was falling asleep; otherwise, Lucien would've kept the room private so he could coax her into a morning romp.

"Lucky dog," he muttered to Taffy.

Taffy didn't seem concerned. Most dogs were seriously intimidated by werewolves. Little dogs tended to shake themselves into pieces if he was anywhere in the near vicinity. But Taffy was different. He was the bookstore corgi. There had always been a bookstore corgi. Lucien wasn't absolutely certain how the corgis came and went over the years, but there had been a different dog here during his childhood. He'd gone away for university and when he'd returned, Taffy had been here. Neither corgi had been afraid of him.

Taffy only made a low, talk-y noise, as if he was a husky, then cuddled close to Amihan's leg, resting his chin on her knee and giving Lucien epic side-eye. Lucien lifted his upper lip and showed the dog some teeth, then tightened his arm around Amihan's waist. Taffy didn't lift his head but did lift a paw onto her leg to press his claim. That was some furry audacity. Lucien let a quiet growl rumble up from his chest.

Amihan groaned, and both Lucien and Taffy froze. She turned onto her back and stretched, her legs straightening, one hand reaching out over the covers to lightly skritch Taffy behind the ears. The little bastard dropped his jaw in a doggie grin, staring straight at Lucien. Then Amihan turned toward Lucien and burrowed deeper against his side under the covers, wrapping the same arm around his waist. Lucien shot a triumphant grin over her shoulder at the corgi before pressing a soft kiss to her temple.

"Are you a coffee or tea person in the morning?" He brushed his lips over the shell of her ear as he asked.

"Food." She rubbed her face in his chest. "There's left-over chicken adobo in the fridge and hot rice in the rice cooker. Food first, then coffee. I like tea later in the afternoon."

"I can make scrambled eggs and toast, if you like." He would have been willing to make her a full English breakfast if they were at his place. The idea of putting a meal in front of her, providing for her, appealed to him.

She nudged her nose up under his jaw before drifting soft kisses on the side of his neck. "Rice and leftover chicken is faster and easier. Less dishes too."

He wouldn't have minded doing them. But then again, his interest in her cooking was piqued. There was going to be more for them to learn about each other, more she definitely needed to know about him.

The full moon was tonight. He had a lot he needed to tell her, and he had to give her time and space to accept it all. It might take months before she would be ready to handle all of who and what he was.

It didn't have to be this full moon. She'd been gone for decades, and now she was back. He could take this slow with her.

A low ring sounded through the room.

Amihan's head shot up so fast, she almost caught his chin.

"Easy." He kept her tucked against his side with one arm as he reached for his phone on her bedside table. "The call is for me."

Whether he would answer it or not would depend on who it was. He was a strong believer in texts unless it was incredibly urgent.

"Mmph." She buried her face in his chest.

He chuckled as he looked at the caller's identity on his phone's screen. Grunting, he accepted the call. "Yeah."

"Lucien," Mel's voice came through and they did not sound happy. "We got an anonymous tip last night. I think you should get a lawyer for Trey and meet us at the station."

Amihan rolled to her back and pulled the covers with her, giving him space to sit up and swing his legs over the edge of the bed. He was growling, he realized, and thankful Amihan didn't seem to be trying to get away from him. He was too close to the full moon to be angry near her before they'd had a chance to talk more. There were things she needed to understand about him.

No time for that now. A pack member needed him. "On my way."

"I'm sorry." Mel shot the apology out just as he ended the call.

Lucien reached for his boxer briefs first, then pulled on his pants. Amihan held the corner of the bedsheet to her front as she sat on the edge of the bed and reached for his clothing, handing him items one at a time.

"Thanks." He really didn't want to leave her, but it was probably for the best at the moment.

"Can I help Trey at all?" Her eyes were wide with concern.

He paused and took her face in both his hands, then kissed her deeply. If he could take her sweet concern with him, he would. When he released her, she had a slightly dazed look, and there was a hint of her arousal scenting the air.

He smirked. "Too many people at the station will only make things complicated. Best thing you can do is work on the bookstore. This is his favorite place in town. There aren't enough safe spaces in the world for any of us, so the bookstore is important. You can get it ready to open and I'll do everything in my power to make sure he's free to walk in."

"Okay." Amihan clenched her jaw with such a look of determination, he couldn't help but feel the surge of energy she inspired.

She was going to get to work, and he had somewhere he needed to be. He hesitated one more time. "This isn't a one-off for me. I'll be back to talk about where this has us as soon as I can."

She nodded and gifted him with a soft smile. "I'm not going anywhere."

A mix of happiness and relief washed through him, easing away a tension he hadn't been ready to acknowledge. He flashed her a grin and then shot down the stairs and out of the bookstore, Taffy barking after him.

As soon as he hit the street, he had his phone out again and was making phone calls. It was early, too early, for most attorneys, but the pack had legal representation from a human that specialized in representing supernaturals. His pack paid enough keeping them on retainer for them to wake the hell up and get to the island posthaste. Until then, Trey would have him.

He walked into the police station to find Mel and their deputy standing in the front office. It was a small building, staffed by just the two of them. Generally, Mel covered the daytime and the deputy worked a portion of the night. They didn't have round-the-clock coverage, but usually the town didn't require it. If there was a problem, calls went to Mel at home. If it was a problem Mel couldn't handle themselves, human or supernatural, the pack or the mayor discreetly provided support.

This morning was different though. The deputy, Brian Saghier, had Trey by the arm. The werewolf had allowed himself to be cuffed with his hands behind his back. Mel's mouth was pressed in a thin line, and the air inside the room smelled of anger and nervousness. All of them had turned toward the front door as Lucien entered.

Mel stepped forward, but it was Brian who spoke. "I followed procedure and read him his rights. I'm placing him in a holding cell and I'll finish my report."

The deputy gripped Trey's arm and pushed the werewolf toward the back room where the holding cells were. He was in a hurry, and his voice was a note or two high for him. The nervousness was coming from him, and he had never seemed particularly uncomfortable with Trey's presence in the past. The two of them didn't interact much, but they'd been in the same local bar for trivia night a couple of times. Lucien didn't like the change in attitude now.

"Wait." Power rolled through the one word, and Lucien didn't particularly care. A human would obey, but they wouldn't necessarily sense or understand why.

Brian blanched. He was a white man of average height and average build with sandy-blond hair and pale-blue eyes. He'd grown up over in Friday Harbor and come to Wolfsound looking for a change of pace that wasn't too different from where he'd come from in the first place. He wasn't aware of the supernaturals living here and hadn't really faced the danger any one of them represented to a human. He hadn't ever given any of them reason to show him in the past. But that didn't mean Lucien was going to allow the human to take any kind of action that would put one of his pack in jeopardy.

"We got an anonymous tip. Trey was spotted near the bookstore after midnight last night, not just in front of it, but snooping around." The words spilled out of Brian's mouth, his tone defensive and pitched even higher than earlier. "He's more than just a regular at the bookstore. Plus, he was there during the fight Declan and Nancy had. Maybe there was something more going on between him and Nancy. He was close enough to Nancy to be a signing witness on the will and all. Maybe he killed Nancy at the bookstore and took her body out to dump at sea. There's nothing to confirm his alibi from the night of the murder either. He must've been returning to the scene of the crime."

"That's enough, Deputy," Mel snapped. "We stick with the facts here, not assumptions."

Brian's mouth shut so hard his teeth clicked. He narrowed his eyes, and red splotches came up over his cheeks and forehead. "We're being professional here, responding to a reasonable complaint. I'm following procedure. Sheriff Altesse was out all day yesterday questioning anyone who had any contact at all with Nan—er, with the victim. That other lady from out of town is cleared. Even with all those weapons, she proved they were historical family heirlooms and centuries old, or something like that. He's our primary suspect and looked to be attempting to break and enter the premises."

Lucien scowled. "I just came from the bookstore. I can tell you no one tried to break and enter all night. I was there."

He'd have to apologize later to Amihan for making their relationship known this way without asking her. He didn't think she'd have a problem with it, but he'd apologize all the same.

Brian's mouth opened and closed a few times before he managed to blurt out more words. "He had an umbrella in his hands and it definitely isn't his. It has a tag saying if found, return to that Matsumoto lady who just moved into town. Really suspicious, lurking around the bookstore with someone else's belongings in hand."

Mel sighed. "Don't take it upon yourself to do anything but what's required for procedure. He's not a transient, so there's no need to give him a shower or a haircut. Just place him in a holding cell and remove his restraints. I'll take it from there. You've been up all night with no sleep."

Lucien didn't want to let Trey out of his sight, but Trey gave him a calm look filled with so much faith, Lucien's anger abated just enough to be under control.

As Trey and Brian left, Mel approached Lucien then,

slow and respectful. Good. This was not the time for Mel to take liberties with their friendship.

Mel turned to Lucien. "I contacted the streaming service Trey uses and haven't received a response to my request for the log-in records to confirm he was using his account to watch those dramas of his. The anonymous tip placed Trey outside the bookstore last night. It's reasonable to question him as to why."

"Is this really enough to make an arrest?" Lucien asked. "Why Trey and not any other suspects?"

"Because he was a close enough friend to sign as a witness in Nancy's will alongside Declan. In homicide cases, it's often somebody the victim knows. Add in his suspicious behavior and he is the primary suspect," Mel said quietly, so low, only Lucien would have been able to hear even if there had been others in the room. "There's massive pressure from the town folk to make an arrest in this murder. I had to take some kind of action."

Lucien settled his gaze on Mel. Brian didn't know who and what he had taken into custody, but Mel did. "It's a full moon tonight. It isn't safe to have any one of us in one of your holding cells on a full moon."

Mel's expression was somber. When they responded, there was nothing but honest truth in their tone, body language, and scent. "I believe that."

CHAPTER

ELEVEN

Amihan had a lot to think about. A lot.

She'd showered after Lucien left, spending a few extra minutes under the steaming hot water to soak the ache out of her muscles. She was sore, in a deliciously wonderful way, and it felt wonderful to take extra care of herself after an amazing night. Happily, the bookstore's water pressure and hot water heater were fantastically able to indulge her. There was a kind of clarity that came with letting her thoughts wander and considerations percolate while taking a long, hot shower.

Afterward, she headed straight downstairs to focus on the world outside the bookstore and the people who were quickly becoming very important to her. Trey was in trouble and sure, Lucien was there doing what he could to help Trey, but she dearly wished she could contribute somehow. But what Lucien had said also made a lot of sense. Ami wasn't a lawyer, and being at the police station herself would only add to the chaos and possibly split Lucien's attention. She wasn't sure what she and Lucien were now, but she didn't want to take up Lucien's energy when they both wanted to help Trey.

So she sat at the register, her gaze sweeping over the book stacks on the main floor and the cloud of tasks in her triage column on the chalkboard. Her traveler's notebook lay open in front of her and her fountain pen lay next to it, ready. She also had her case open, with her other pens and one of her favorite inks—the Oxblood—in it. It was a gorgeous color that worked well on a variety of papers, from actual quality notebook paper intended for use with fine pens to sticky notes. It generally didn't feather or bleed through, and it dried fairly quickly, which was a major consideration for a lefty like her. Then again, she liked to use fine nib tips with her fountain pens so less ink flowed out onto whatever paper she was using. A whole drop would bleed through even thicker paper.

An image surfaced in her mind of her own blood welling up from her fingertip, the drop falling here onto the counter. Onto paper.

It had been Nancy's last will and testament.

Ami pulled out her phone and swiped though the images. She hadn't really paid a lot of attention to it because she hadn't known Nancy well and figured the only aspect of the will pertinent to herself was the bookstore. The will transferred ownership of The Mystic Bookstore to the Scribe, an individual to be recognized by the three town elders and . . . Taffy. Well, that was quirky. Ami wasn't even sure how that would hold up in court if anyone were to challenge it.

But there had been another specific bequest. It was only listed as "the unsINKable" and the will stated that it should be returned to its previous owner. But what was it?

Ami jumped to her feet, then ran upstairs, almost stumbling as she kicked off her boots at the landing. She rushed to the master bedroom, her socks sliding on the hardwood floors. There had been framed photos in there. She'd barely looked, feeling she was intruding on Nancy's personal life and unsure whether family would show up to collect the former bookstore owner's personal effects.

There, on a dresser, was a photo of Nancy and a man down at the harbor. They were standing in front of a boat. Its name wasn't unusual, but how it was spelled was: the unsINKable.

It wasn't listed in the places investigated. It hadn't been mentioned in any of Mel's notes. It belonged to Nancy, though, and had been worth listing as a special bequest. It was worth checking out, for sure. It might even be on Mel's list of things to look into, just lower in priority than talking to actual persons of interest.

Lucien and Mel were busy dealing with the situation around Trey, and she didn't want to distract them from that. The less time Trey had to spend waiting for things to resolve, the better. So it might be best to let them concentrate on the situation at the police station and wait for Lucien to let her know how things had worked out.

Finally, she decided to text Mel to bring their attention to the special bequest in the will. Perhaps Mel knew already and hadn't mentioned it. So it might not be all that important a discovery.

Amihan wandered back downstairs. Taffy followed close at her heels, watching her intently. She sat behind the register, looking at her to-do sticky notes.

"I just need to find the inventory lists and so long as the legal stuff is settled, there's not a whole lot keeping me from opening for business." She made the statement out loud, tasting the truth of it.

On a hunch, she opened the drawer under the register where she'd found the will the first night. There, in the drawer, where there hadn't been anything before, was a neat stack of papers. She took them out and scanned them. The book inventory list was a little old-fashioned, but it had the basic data. The bookstore only had one copy of most of the books, maybe two or three of what she guessed were popular books.

"No time like the present to get to know where all the genres are." She hopped off the stool and then, starting at the far bookcase, got a feel for the current layout of the bookstore.

The inventory list was accurate, of course. She still spent a lot of time checking each bookshelf, looking for anything that might need immediate repair. She also pondered whether it would make sense to rearrange anything. Restlessness nibbled at the edges of her thoughts, and she struggled to stay on task.

Still, she managed to use up hours making certain she was intimately familiar with the bookstore and where everything was in it. After lunch she even pulled out her laptop and started to set up a digital inventory. She wasn't certain the bookstore would be able to interact with it, but she thought it would make a lot of sense to update the inventory system. Maybe she'd design a website too.

Really, Nancy had left the bookstore in good order. Sure, there was some renovation Amihan might want to do, but none of it had to happen immediately. It could be done little by little as she continued to get to know the bookstore and the spaces inside it. She thought about the reading room downstairs and the information organized on the wall. She'd honestly been waiting for closure on Nancy's death. There wasn't anything that absolutely had to be done to get the bookstore ready. It was that she needed to be ready.

Her thoughts kept returning to the boat in the photo upstairs. It had looked like it was right in the harbor here in Wolfsound. Could it be easy to find?

She looked at Taffy. "How about a walk?"

Taffy let out one happy bark and trotted to the back door. A hook had appeared next to the door and a leash was hanging from it. She was certain she'd left Taffy's leash at the front, but hey, magic bookstore. Taffy was also a magic bookstore corgi, so who knew what else might be possible?

"Let's go be curious together." She hooked the leash to Taffy's collar and took him out the front door, sliding her hand over the doorframe as she went. "We'll be back soon."

Twenty minutes later, she and Taffy were wandering the harbor area and the small marina. There were four docks or piers stretching out into the harbor, with many narrower finger piers extending perpendicular to those bigger walkways. There were plenty of boats of various sizes in the marina. A few people waved at her and Taffy as they walked up and down the area. It took maybe an hour, but they found it. The unsINKable.

She didn't know much about boats, so she had no idea if it was considered big or small. It was far from the largest boat in the marina, and it was equally not the smallest. It had a sort of cockpit, and there was a rather spacious seating area in the forward part of the boat.

She looked around and no one was in the vicinity. It felt like the marina had emptied just in time for dinner.

"No one would get upset if I took a closer look, right?"

Taffy only gave her a puzzled look, his head tilted to one side.

"You stay here. I've no idea if you can swim, but let's not find out today, okay? Stay."

She dropped Taffy's leash and the corgi sat. She figured that was as clear an indication as any that Taffy was going to obey. She made a mental note to start going over training commands with Taffy. Mealtimes were probably good for that. Taffy seemed pretty food driven.

Stepping onto the boat was an awkward moment. It wasn't stationary exactly. It floated on the water, and the water was not a perfectly still surface. She managed to get on without stumbling or falling, though, so that was a win. Next, she poked around.

There was very little out in the open. Everything seemed to be neatly stowed, each thing having its own place. One compartment in the cockpit held papers in a plastic storage bag. Among them was a certificate of sale for the boat.

"Oh, this makes things more complicated for Trey," Ami muttered.

She didn't take the certificate out, but she did take a photo with her phone. She hadn't remembered to charge it earlier and it was at low battery now. She really should get back to the bookstore.

There was some kind of bulky thing covered in a tarp at the back end. Of course, she peeked. It was a motor, and it seemed to have been pulled up somehow so it was out of the water. There were dark stains on the blades of the propeller. It was obvious someone had tried to wipe them clean, but there was still gunk in harder-to-reach spots. It was just too reddish-black to be mud. She pulled out her phone and took a few pictures.

"What are you doing, Amihan?" The question was low and deep, growly.

She popped up from under the tarp and whipped around to face the voice. Lucien stood there in the dimming evening. He did not look happy.

TWELVE

L ucien waited for Amihan's answer, not daring to come closer while worry and concern fed the raging wildness inside him. The sun was setting and the moon was rising. His control had thinned out to threads. It was a risk to be here, to be near, yes. But he'd wanted to check in with her, and when she wasn't at the bookstore, he'd needed to know where she'd gone, assure himself she was safe. Alone out here, on a boat that smelled of ill intentions and suspicious people, was not safe.

"This boat was in a photograph of Nancy and Declan Simpa." Amihan's words were steady and delivered with a heavy dose of caution. "It wasn't mentioned anywhere in the notes we'd gone over with Mel and I thought it would be worth checking out."

Fair. Totally reasonable. He rolled his shoulders and stretched his neck, his vertebrae popping with the released tension. He realized he was clenching his hands into fists and made the effort to relax them too. He was doing his best to hold on to rational thought for as long as he could.

He swallowed hard, looking at her. "Even with Trey

making things more suspicious for himself, there wasn't enough concrete evidence to arrest him. Mel was able to release Trey into the custody of the pack lawyer. I was able to send Trey out of harm's way with the rest of the pack, inside the state park."

She was beautiful in the waning light. Her skin glowed, and the burnt umber of her eyes was ignited by all the colors of the sunset. Her soft lips were parted slightly as she stared at him, and he could see himself reflected in her eyes.

"I went to the bookstore to check in with you before I left for the night too," he continued. It might be too soon to explain everything to her. He hadn't wanted to overwhelm her or scare her away, but he also hadn't wanted to keep anything from her. "But you were gone. I tracked you here, just to make sure you were okay. This is not a good place to be."

"Let's not make tracking me places a habit." She scowled at him.

He scowled right back. "There's a murderer loose."

"You have a point." She still crossed her arms over her chest.

"But yes, fine." He ground out his agreement. "For right now we can talk about how you're standing on a dodgy boat with the sun going down."

"About that." Amihan lifted her phone and waved it. "I found some papers here and they make things even more confusing, maybe."

He narrowed his eyes. Her scent was sharp, and her posture was slightly hunched. It could have been because of the rocking boat. He didn't think she was used to finding her balance on a deck like this. It could also be because she didn't want to tell him what she knew. But this was

Amihan, and he was learning that she wasn't one to avoid a thing even if she didn't want to do it.

"There's a certificate of sale here, indicating this boat used to belong to Trey. He sold it to Declan." Amihan pressed her lips together.

That added one more tie between Trey and Nancy and Declan. Trey had said he hadn't killed Nancy, and Lucien hadn't smelled a lie. This was one more thing they'd need to counter as they strove to prove Trey's innocence from the perspective of human law.

"But there's a sticky note on it too." Amihan used her fingertips to zoom in on the photo she had on her phone. "It's theoretically from Trey. We'll have to match it to a sample of his handwriting. Wishing Nancy all the fun learning to boat with her boyfriend. Says shared hobbies like this can bring new life to a relationship on the rocks."

Lucien grunted. "Not so perfect a relationship between Nancy and Declan, then."

"Apparently not, and wait, there's more." Amihan sounded like she was trying to make a joke, but her voice was strained. He didn't like it when she was distressed.

Lucien stilled. He tried to make his voice as calm as possible. "What is it, Amihan?"

She lifted the tarp. "Is this what I think it is? Is this the kind of thing Mel sent you to check for around the other suspects?"

The boat continued to rock as silence fell between them for long moments. He didn't move, couldn't get too close to her as anxiety and anger started to rise up and twist around inside him. "This boat smells of old blood and anger and desperation. You shouldn't be here."

"Then this is blood? Because I'm pretty sure there's

fabric caught up around part of this thing too." Amihan pushed for clarification, and he snarled in frustration.

Her eyes widened and she stilled. Maybe it was instinctive, and that was good, but his fraying composure was a warning neither of them could ignore. There was a roaring in his ears as he struggled to hold on to his human form as long as possible.

He took in a deep breath, thankful that the unique combination of sweet florals and earthy spice in her scent grounded him. He took a step toward her and caught himself. She had asked him a question, requested something from him. He could give her what she wanted. Something slid into place inside him as he came to that conclusion.

He moved to stand next to her and bent to take a whiff of what was under the tarp, careful not to touch her. If he did, he'd wrap his arms around her and pull her to him and bury his nose in her hair. This was not the place. It wasn't a wise time. She'd asked him a question.

"Yes, that's blood." His voice came out rough.

He looked down at her. This close, she had to tilt her head back to look up at him. Her pupils had widened and her scent heated. She was aware of his proximity in a way that made his lips curve into a smug smile.

"Do you think this is the primary crime scene Mel was looking for?" Her question came out a little breathy.

He liked that too. Then his brain processed what she'd asked him.

He scowled. "If it is, you definitely shouldn't be here and absolutely shouldn't have come here alone."

Her jaw tightened and her eyes narrowed. "I had perfectly good reasoning for coming down here to check out a hunch. You could ask me what that was. I didn't come here alone either. Taffy is with me."

"Taffy is not on this boat." He lifted his upper lip, snarling again. "And Taffy is great for friendly company, insufficient for protection."

"Taffy is very brave—" She glanced to the side and her eyes widened.

He turned to look in the same direction as her.

"—and a lot farther away than I realized," she finished on a whisper. "Where is he?"

Damn it. He'd been too focused on her, egregious error on his part. Taffy was nowhere to be seen or scented. Worse, someone had managed to untie the dock lines, and the current was carrying them out and away from the marina. They weren't far yet, but far enough that he couldn't make a jump from the boat to the dock. If he couldn't, with his enhanced athleticism, Amihan definitely couldn't.

He pondered the distance, wondering if he could throw her.

She was moving, and his attention snapped to her again. She was poking at the cockpit controls. "Nothing seems to be working. I'm not sure I know how to use anything, but I thought a radio or something would be here. There's literally no power."

He joined her. It was fairly easy to identify the communications unit situated to one side of the control area with a coiled cord leading to a handheld mic. The display showed nothing, even when Amihan flipped up the tiny red button cover labeled Distress and pressed the button. He didn't try to do it, trusting her to operate delicate equipment at a time when all he wanted to do was bash and pound at the control panel in the cockpit until it sparked into response.

Whatever somewhat-rational portion of his brain remained recognized that force would not work in this instance.

"Someone's going to notice there's a boat adrift in the harbor." She was scanning the shores, probably looking for anyone to wave at for help. "What are the odds this boat is absolutely out of power?"

"Has to be deliberate." He started searching for some kind of emergency kit, anything that might have flares or some other way to signal for aid. "You're going to need help soon. The sun has set and the full moon is rising."

"Is that bad?" Amihan's voice was still calm, but there was a thread of tension now.

He stopped his rummaging and straightened to face her. "I was going to stay away tonight. Give you some time to get used to me when I have control over who and what I am. Talk you through what it means to live as a werewolf so you'd know who you were getting involved with."

His voice sounded rough, even to his ears. At least he could still speak. Some of the pack had already changed to answer the moon's call earlier in the afternoon. There weren't many of them on the island. They would be drawn to him, but his father would keep them within the bounds of the state park where they wouldn't be in danger of discovery. The pack still had a leader to look after them if he wasn't there. This time. He needed to be smarter in the future.

But this woman unhinged him, and now, she might pay a terrible price.

"I'm going to change, Amihan." He did his best to express the urgency of the situation. "I have to answer the moon's call and I will change. I'm going to be bigger than a wolf and I am much more dangerous. And you are trapped here on this boat with me."

Her eyes went wide. She leaned back against the cockpit, and gripped the steering wheel so tight, her knuckles were pale beneath her skin. "We could try to swim to shore. It's not that far. It'd be hard against the current but we're both healthy adults."

He shook his head. "This time of year, open water swimming is tough even for experienced swimmers. Neither of us has any kind of gear to help us maintain body heat to swim that far without any kind of conditioning. A human wouldn't make it. You'd succumb to hypothermia in minutes if the shock of the cold water doesn't take you down in seconds."

"What about you? Could you make it to shore and get someplace safe?" she asked.

He almost smiled, despite the situation. She wasn't asking him to get someplace safe for others. She was concerned for him. "When I change form, I won't be able to swim. Werewolves are lean with too much muscle and bone density to swim. We just sink. I'd drown."

She looked at the motor. "We don't know if this motor works without power to the cockpit, but if we put it in the water and try, we might lose the evidence."

They both fell silent. Lucien racked his brain for a solution. She started looking around for an emergency kit in case he missed it and pulled an orange case from a compartment. When she opened it, it was empty.

"This is looking more and more suspicious," he muttered. If he harmed her, if the worst happened, he would make sure to hunt down the person responsible for this before he did penance for his actions.

She swallowed hard. "What would you have done if you'd had time to talk me through what would happen, get me used to the idea?"

He stared hard at her.

She lifted her chin and met his gaze.

"It wouldn't have been anywhere near a full moon." He could answer her when she asked him a question. It helped steady him. "The change hurts. You should do your best not to touch me as I'm going through it. It's hard to watch and I understand if you can't, but I would want you to understand the entirety of what I go through as a werewolf."

She was brave. So brave. Even now, with his impending transformation, she wasn't afraid. This night, if she survived it, might teach her to be afraid of him, and he didn't want that.

He swallowed hard and continued. "After I'm done, let me come to you. Don't stare into my eyes, not right away. We have to work up to that so I don't perceive you as challenging or threatening me. Try not to move or make any sudden gestures."

"Okay," she whispered. Her voice was soft, soothing.

"On a full moon, I'm not rational. I'm acting completely on instinct and I'm extremely reactive. I won't be thinking like a human." He struggled to give her actionable instructions, not just information. "If you talk to me, try to stay calm. No shouting. Try not to be afraid of me. The worst thing you can do is try to run from me."

She huffed out a faint laugh. "I'm not going anywhere."

He searched her expression for some sign of what she was thinking, how she was taking any of this. The ache was starting in his joints, and his skin had grown hot and sensitive. He started to strip. He needed to minimize the irritation he experienced so his wolf form would be as calm as possible. On a boat, surrounded by deep water. Damn it. He wasn't going to be calm at all.

She might not survive this.

He wouldn't survive if he came back to his human senses and found her dead because of him.

"I'll get off the boat." It was the best decision.

Her whole body jerked. "What? No."

He moved to the side of the boat in two steps. "Better one of us than both of us. I lost my shit as a kid seeing you hurt once. I've carried the guilt all these years. I couldn't bear it if I killed you tonight. I'd rather choose this way to end it than live through that."

"No." Amihan closed the distance between them and put a hand on his forearm.

He snarled, and as he did, he felt his jaws extend forward, beginning their transformation into a muzzle.

She lifted her hand slowly and showed him both her hands, palms out. "Stay, Lucien. Please stay with me."

CHAPTER

THIRTEEN

Amihan watched Lucien's eyes turn to liquid silver as he glared at her. Slowly, he turned away from the side of the boat and toward her. His snarling subsided.

She backed away from him one step at a time, giving him space. The moon was rising out over the harbor, appearing impossibly big as it lifted above the horizon.

He didn't say anything more. Instead, he ripped his clothes off, with fingers curved into claws. His body was already changing. She remembered the sculpted, lean body he had earlier in the day. She'd gotten to know him intimately.

Now, his tendons were standing out against his skin, and his body was covered in sweat. Naked, he crouched down in front of her. He groaned in pain. His back bowed as joints popped, and a grinding sound made her wonder if bone was rubbing against bone.

It was hard to watch. She had never been a horror or gore movie fan. But this was Lucien, and he'd said he wanted her to understand what werewolves went through.

There was so much pain in this. Her heart ached for him and for Trey.

Minutes ticked by. She didn't know how many. Time felt elastic, then Lucien stood before her on four legs, covered in fur. He hadn't been kidding. She'd only ever seen pictures and videos of wolves, but he was far bigger than any of those.

His face was all wolf, and he had a powerful set of jaws. His lips curled briefly, flashing huge canine teeth. His ears swiveled forward as he stood stiff-legged, his tail straight out behind him.

She hunched her shoulders instinctively, not crouching down, but definitely not trying to stand nose to nose with him. Awe had numbed her, which was kind of a good thing. She had the impression that it would've been bad for her to be afraid. She didn't want to fear him.

His fur was white and silver in the light of the full moon, with a few hints of black. It was longer and thicker around his neck and shoulders. His legs weren't slender like a husky's. They were thicker and seemed powerful to her. His paws were as big as her hands with her fingers outstretched.

There was barely enough room for him to stand on the boat—he was as tall as her. She tried not to think about his jaws or his teeth, but she was really very glad she wasn't wearing a red hoodie.

The floorboards of the boat creaked as he stepped toward her. Her gaze had fallen away from his face as she'd taken in the rest of his form. She figured it might be wise to center her focus on his chest.

He was panting, and she didn't know if that was normal for him. It could be from pain or from exertion. She had no idea. But he moved to stand close enough to her that his pants blew hot air across her face and neck. Nervousness fluttered through her chest and into her belly.

Abruptly, she realized she'd been standing a long time. It might have been a smarter idea to have taken a seat all the way at the back of the boat, as out of the way as possible. Her knees felt wobbly, and she figured it would be bad if she crumpled to the floor now. Lucien had told her to try not to make sudden moves.

The werewolf hadn't killed her yet, though. If she could follow Lucien's instructions, they might get through this.

His huge muzzle extended toward her until his black nose hovered just in front of her face. The sound of his sniffing was loud in her ears. She did her best to hold still, but the boat was swaying and so was she. His nose dropped lower, to her neck and over her chest, then he bumped her.

She tried to step back and catch herself, but she hadn't looked behind her so her right foot caught on something and she rolled her ankle. Pain shot up her right leg and she bit her lip, doing her best to swallow her surprised cry as her leg buckled and she sat back.

Luckily, she caught the edge of the seat and sat into it, getting her weight off her leg as fast as she could. She squeezed her eyes shut. Lucien had snarled as she tripped and fell, and now his growl was a steady rumble in his chest. He hadn't moved though—hadn't done anything violent.

He had told her to do her best not to be frightened of him. She counted to ten in her head, first in Thai, then in Tagalog, then in English. With each set of ten, she forced her major muscle groups to relax as best she could. She started at her toes and moved up her legs, cataloging the pain in her right ankle as she went, then went to her hands and arms, and continued to her core and shoulders and even her face. By the time she finished her third iteration, she had a firm grasp on her calm and Lucien's nose was back, snuffling her.

"Lucien," she whispered.

The sniffing paused, but no snarl or growl came.

She thought it might be good to continue. "Lucien, I'm okay. I'm guessing you're okay. We can get through this."

He moved and the boat shifted under him. A growl rose up from his chest, and his lips lifted to reveal teeth. Not good.

"Steady." She tilted her head, looking up at his ears. They felt less threatening than the teeth. She tried not to think about how close they were. "It's good I'm sitting now. Maybe you should sit or lie down too. It'd rock the boat less."

He'd said he wouldn't be thinking like a human. But she hoped he would respond to her voice, so she tried for a soothing tone. His growling grew quieter so she thought he was listening.

She continued to murmur soft suggestions, giving him a stream of consciousness because it helped her reduce her anxiousness and gave him something to listen to. His ears were twitching as she spoke, the way Taffy's did when the corgi was listening to her. It seemed like Lucien was too.

"I know I was hoping someone would see us before to come help," she said wistfully, "but now I'm really not sure it'd be a good idea for anyone to come by until you've had a chance to change back. I honestly don't have a clue when that will be."

Lucien finally huffed and lowered himself to his belly with a grunt, leaning his head to mostly lie in her lap.

She froze. Okay, then. It took another round of counting

to ten in three different languages to slow her heart rate down.

She had always thought meeting a real wolf in one of those facilitated interactions would be full of wonder. And there was wonder, definitely. There was also a hefty dose of wary intimidation when it came to Lucien.

There was an aura about him that wasn't of the world she knew. It had been one thing for him to tell her he was a werewolf, for him to growl and exude his Mr. Supernaturally Grumpy energy. It was another thing completely to have watched him turn into a giant wolf that was more than a wolf.

Still, this was magic. More real to her than the subtle actions of a mystical bookstore or a talking tortoise. This was Lucien, and somehow he had become very central to her thoughts and feelings.

"You're gorgeous." It was probably better to tell him in this form than to admit it when he was human and have to face his insufferable smirk. He took smug to a whole new level.

She had no desire to run from him. Just as well, because her right ankle was swelling and she wasn't going to be walking, let alone running, anywhere fast once they could get up and out of this boat. But she did want to talk to him. So she did.

"I was going to ask you where the two of us were going, when we had a chance to talk." She kept her voice low and soothing, like before. "Like, are we in a relationship? We're in something. And maybe it doesn't need to be defined, but I wonder what even is a relationship to a werewolf?"

Because honestly, those questions had been hovering at the edge of her mind all day. Was she allowed to tell her friends about him? About him being a werewolf? She'd been dying to text Helen that something had happened last night.

Text Helen. Text. She still had her phone. How could she not have thought of it? Lucien had been preoccupied and not quite in full use of the human aspect of his mental faculties, fine. But she had no such excuse. She'd have face-palmed if the sudden movement wouldn't risk unwanted reaction in Lucien.

Ami moved as slow as she could and pulled her phone out of her pocket. Lucien opened one eye to watch her, then lifted his head. He sniffed her hand and the phone, but when nothing happened, he settled his head back down on her lap.

She let out a breath she'd been holding and checked her phone. No signal. They must be too far out on the water. And if her battery was low before, it was close to dead now. She turned off her phone to conserve battery.

No phone. No power on the boat. No flashlight or flare or anything. Honestly, with Lucien like this, she didn't want anyone to come out to them anyway. Not until he changed back. Maybe she could make some kind of flag out of what was left of his clothes and wave down help in the morning.

She looked around. It was a beautiful night. She was alive. Lucien was freaking magnificent. He'd be magnificently naked when he changed back too.

Maybe all she had to do was problem-solve how to hold her bladder for however many hours it was going to be.

FOURTEEN

Lucien stood in the corner of the front room at the police station, his arms crossed over his chest. A pack member had come by with a change of clothes, so he had at least been able to change out of the spare jogging suit Mel had brought him when they'd come out with the harbor's only towboat.

"It's a good thing Taffy showed up before I left the office," Mel was saying. "He led me out to the marina and I saw the boat out there. I realized it'd be a bad idea to bring you both in with the moon rising, so I made sure no one would go out there to get you until morning."

Lucien scowled, but Mel was mostly talking to Amihan anyway.

"Bridget, Det, and Jin are cooking up some story about a romantic moonlight cruise date between the two of you. They plan to post it on the town social media. Figured romance was the perfect distraction for anyone who saw you out there asking questions."

Lucien had several questions of his own that needed to

be answered in the next few minutes, and maybe one or two he was afraid to ask.

Amihan sat in the chair behind Mel's desk, wrapped in a blanket, her right foot elevated on a second chair. He had no memory of how she'd been injured, and the only other being on the boat with her had been him.

She was hurt. She was hurt. She was hurt. Again. He'd been there with her. Again.

"Sheriff, I came as soon as I got your message." Deputy Saghier burst into the police station, his uniform shirt only half buttoned, his hair not yet brushed. "We're making an arrest this morning?"

The man sounded excited, but he stopped short as he caught sight of Amihan. Lucien watched and waited. It was a touch of his magic to go unnoticed in plain sight. As long as he didn't move, his presence blended into his surroundings—ever the patient predator.

"Miss . . . er . . . Ami, what happened? Do you need to go to a hospital? Or do you need to file a report?" At least Saghier had the decency to be concerned.

Mel tapped their desk, drawing Saghier's attention to them. "Yes, we're making an arrest today. I'm just waiting on one more person, then we can—"

"Was it really necessary to insist I come down to the station?" Declan Simpa entered without knocking. He strode right in and slapped his baseball cap down on the edge of the deputy's desk. "I have soccer club activities this morning."

"You weren't happy the other day when I came to question you after practice, Declan, so I would think you'd appreciate coming here directly." Mel was smooth today, all cool confidence and comfort in their authority as the town sheriff. Lucien could smell the anger radiating off them, but it wasn't readily apparent in their relaxed facial expression or body language.

"Oh, well, what did you want then?" The wind had been taken out of Simpa's sails, and the man stood there, uncertain, rolling his baseball cap into a fabric burrito.

"I know we already searched the boat attached to your business." Mel lifted a set of papers they had waiting on their own desk, making a show of looking at them. "But we weren't aware of this one."

"Right well, you're welcome to check around. It's just been down at the marina this whole time." Simpa was pale under his tan. "I've got nothing to hide."

Lucien almost laughed. The first statement had been truthful, but the last statement literally stank of the man's lie.

"I can head down to the marina right now and check it out," Saghier offered. "That's why you called me in, I guess."

Lucien didn't think he'd ever heard the deputy so eager to do work outside his usual shift.

Mel waved the sheets of paper in their hand. "We recovered a boat this morning and checked the owner registration. Seems it belonged to you and we wanted to let you know it was towed in."

Simpa walked closer to Mel. He had to in order to take the papers from them. "That so?"

"It's the primary crime scene, we're certain of it." Mel had brought them in, the trap was closing in on them.

Simpa's gaze went straight to Saghier as he laughed nervously. "What is this? You can't be thinking I killed Nancy? I was here all night."

"Were you?" Mel brandished the papers. "We had to send some samples we found on the boat to the lab, so I sent along a couple of other items that were confusing us. Like your clothes from that night. Lucky we found those in a duffel on your back doorstep. Funny though, they weren't there the other day. They showed up just last night."

The papers were just confirmation of receipts. It was too soon to have actual DNA results back. Lucien and Mel both knew it. Amihan was keeping silent, but Lucien thought she probably knew it too.

Saghier and Simpa were taking turns glancing at the nearest exit and each other. Their reactions told almost as much as the actual DNA results would have.

"We'll get to that in a moment." Mel laid one sheet of paper down, pulling their attention back to them. "There were blood, tissue, and fibers on the motor on the unsINKable, the boat we towed in this morning. Nancy's body was all cut up. No sea animal did that. She died falling or being thrown off that boat. The only other signs of people on that boat were fingerprints and hair matching the color of yours, Declan, or that of the person who found the boat last night."

Good. No need to mention Ami's name if it wasn't necessary. Mel was creating a story out of facts and guesses, letting the listeners fill in the gaps with their own guilty consciences.

Saghier cleared his throat. "But that doesn't necessarily mean—"

"It was the bookstore, wasn't it." Declan was staring at Ami, despite Mel not having mentioned her name. "Nancy said the bookstore was some kind of magical thing. You're the new bookstore owner. You're here now. I bet the bookstore told you or something. It knows I did it."

Lucien traded glances with Mel. This wasn't how they thought this was going to go down.

Declan laughed, the sound unsteady and full of paranoia. "I didn't plan it. Nothing went the way I planned."

He pulled a chain at his neck so it lay out on his shirt. A ring hung on the simple chain. "I proposed to her that day, asked her to come away with me. She said no. She said she loved me but she said no to me anyway. You want to know why? Because of that cursed and haunted bookstore."

Saghier was shaking his head slowly, his mouth forming the word *no*.

Amihan tipped her head slightly to one side, her eyes wide as she blinked. Usually, it was a cute habit of hers. This time, it was deliberate, with an almost-creepy doll effect.

Declan shuddered as he stared at her. "Haunted. Definitely. So I tried to set her free. I tried to burn the place down."

Well, that answered the question of who attempted arson that night.

Declan was wringing the baseball cap in his hands like a rag. "But then that Japanese lady showed and wind blew up from nowhere, putting the fire out like it was nothing but a candle on a birthday cake."

"She has a name," Amihan snapped. Mel blinked and Lucien tensed, but Declan ignored her.

"No one would believe me. Who could? I didn't believe what I saw." Declan shook his head. "Her and her weird fan with those creepy umbrellas hopping around at her feet. I got good and drunk that night and you all arrested me like I was the one who ought to be locked up."

Amihan straightened in her seat but didn't say more. Lucien narrowed his eyes.

Trey had been spotted around the outside of the bookstore because there had been a red umbrella in the doorway and it had rolled into the shadows next to the building rather unnaturally. Trey had gone after it in case it had been a danger to Amihan. It looked like he needed to have a talk with Matsumoto Rio about umbrellas that weren't what they seemed.

"You phoned in the anonymous tip." Lucien said quietly.

"Course I did. Called from the bar." Declan spat out the admission. "Wasn't natural. None of it."

"What else did you do, Declan?" Mel asked, their tone equally as quiet as Lucien's had been.

"I needed to get Nancy out of there." Declan was escalating in volume as he became more agitated. He looked around and his gaze caught on the deputy. "Saghier was the only one who understood that what I wanted was in Nancy's best interest. He let me out, switched clothes with me, so the cameras in the cell would show somebody here all night. He let me go to Nancy."

"Wait a minute . . ." Saghier made a move to grab Declan, but Mel drew their weapon and shook their head. Saghier blanched and stayed where he was.

Might have been the first time a sheriff had drawn their weapon in years. This was a small, sleepy town. Declan wasn't paying attention to Mel's weapon though. Instead, he'd locked onto Amihan. Lucien didn't like that, but he waited. He was close enough to intercede if Declan made a move toward her.

"I found Nancy near the bookstore, assessing the damage outside." Declan's voice was strained. "I took her with me down to the unsINKable. She acted like she didn't want to come, but I thought it was because the bookstore could hear."

Amihan's posture had changed. She was leaning

forward slightly, her expression one of earnest interest. "Why the unsINKable?"

Her tone was sweet, curious. Declan responded to her in a way he hadn't earlier. Everyone liked an avid listener.

"We'd bought it together. The boat," Declan said. "Yeah it was registered under my name, I insisted. But it was ours together. It was supposed to fix us."

His hand was shaking as he took the ring in his hand and made a fist around it.

"I got Nancy on board and cast off. It's just a bowrider, not really made for the distance, but it would've gotten us to the place I rented for us on the mainland. I had to empty out the emergency kit so she couldn't use a flare or anything to signal for help." His voice fell to a whisper. "We could've gone from there to anywhere. It would've been just us."

"Wait!" Saghier shouted, and Ami jumped at the shift in volume. "You weren't going to come back? You promised you'd come back. I've been keeping my mouth shut this entire time, covering for your sorry ass because you promised."

Declan's face twisted into a sneer. "Whatever. You can find your own job with a real police station on the mainland. You rely too much on people who know people to get you what you want."

Saghier spluttered, but didn't move.

Declan groaned. "Does it matter? It doesn't matter. None of it does. I took the boat out of the harbor and it was fine. Everything was going to be fine. We went beyond the bay and were well into the sound. It wouldn't have been long before we'd cleared the islands and reached the mainland."

"But Nancy had a life here," Lucien said, unwilling to let

Amihan draw Declan's attention again. "She had the bookstore."

Declan glared at Lucien, a wild look in his eyes. "I was saving her. Sure Nancy was crying and begging me to go back. Sure. But once I showed her the nice place I'd set up for us, she would have given it a chance."

"What happened next, Declan?" Mel asked, drawing Declan's attention.

"She wouldn't stop crying about the damned bookstore!" Declan shouted. "She was going to make herself sick with all the sobbing, so I grabbed her and shook her. I shook her and shook her but she started screaming."

Amihan had covered her mouth with her hands.

"Don't look at me like that," Declan snarled. "Sound carries over the water so I put my hands around Nancy's neck to make her be quiet. It was her fault. She wouldn't be quiet. She wouldn't just come with me and be with me. She wouldn't. So I made her be quiet."

There was silence in the room. Every one of them was staring at him, and Declan moved to look at each one of them in turn. The anger seeped out of him.

"When I realized. Well, it was too late, wasn't it?" Declan laughed and the sound came out high-pitched and wrong. "I let her fall overboard and she got pulled under the boat. The . . . the propellers made a sound and I . . . I knew. It was over. I just knew. So I brought the boat around and came back to the marina. I docked the boat and tried to wipe the propellors as best I could. I couldn't see anything that anyone else would find, so I covered it with a tarp and came back up."

Even Saghier was staring, his mouth hanging open.

Declan continued to whisper. "No one knew. No one

saw. No one could've known. So it had to be the bookstore. The bookstore knew she died and it knew I did it."

The man was crying by then. Tears streamed down his face, and his nose was running. His face was contorted, and he clutched at the ring on the chain around his neck. Between sobs, he muttered, "It knew. It knew."

Mel finally spoke. "Lucien, I'm deputizing you for the moment. Please take Declan Simpa and Brian Saghier into custody while I read them their rights."

CHAPTER
FIFTEEN

"I can't believe you carried me all the way here," Ami muttered. Her face was burning with embarrassment, and she covered her face with her hands.

Lucien chuckled, the sound rolling up from his chest. She felt it as well as heard it, pressed as she was to him as he cradled her in his arms.

"This is the cutest picture!" Bridget exclaimed from across the street. "I'm posting it to the town socials right now!"

Ami groaned. "I haven't even been here a week."

The bookstore door opened inward before Lucien even tried to get the doorknob. Lucien took it in stride and carried her straight inside. A happy bark greeted them. Taffy came scampering down from upstairs, then danced around Lucien's feet in an attempt to reach Ami.

"You've had a rough night. Let me get you settled so you can finally get some real rest." Lucien continued through the bookstore and up the stairs.

"Shoes," Ami whispered, but it was unnecessary.

He paused at the landing and toed off his shoes. Then

he carried her right into the guest room. He helped ease her boot off her swollen right foot, scowling. "This is going to swell up even more. Your boot was providing some compression. It was the right decision to keep it on until now. Let me help you out of your pants, then get some ice on this ankle."

She wanted to make a clever remark, something witty about him helping her out of her pants, but she couldn't think of anything. Plus, it didn't feel right. Something was off between them. His brows were still drawn together and his lips pressed in a thin line. Most of all, he wouldn't look her in the eyes.

In minutes, he had her tucked into her bed, her right foot propped up on pillows, an ice pack loosely wrapped around her ankle. She hadn't had an ice pack in the freezer, but he'd found one. She was going to need to figure out what else the bookstore could provide and whether there were any rules to it all. Even magic had to have limitations and rules of some sort.

But all of that could wait for another day.

"Well, I'll let you get some rest." Lucien backed away from the bed.

Alarm shot through Ami. This wasn't just him taking a couple of physical steps away. "Wait."

Lucien stopped inside the doorway. He still wouldn't make eye contact.

"What is happening right now?" She asked, trying hard not to let the tremble she felt in her chest come out in her words. "There's a lot we need to talk about, between last night and the night before. A lot. Can't we talk about at least some of it?"

He closed his eyes, and his shoulders slumped. "You're hurt. Again."

Again?

Ami shook her head. "Lucien. This isn't your fault."

"I was the only one with you." His voice was deep, rough, full of emotion. He let out a single bark of laughter, devoid of any kind of happiness. "I should be grateful it wasn't worse. I could've killed you. The only difference between me and Declan? It would've been my teeth and my claws ripping you to shreds, instead of the boat propellors."

"You didn't." Ami put every ounce of force she could muster behind her voice, filling her words with intensity rather than shouting. "You changed and you sniffed and then you laid down. That was it. You didn't threaten me in any way."

Well, there'd been some snarling and growling, but Lucien had been in pain.

Lucien's gaze caught her then, and his silver-grey eyes searched her for any hint of a lie. "How did you get hurt, Amihan?"

Embarrassment came back, heating her cheeks, and if her next words came out a little grumpy, she figured she had a right to it. "I tripped. Backwards. I stepped back and rolled my ankle over nothing, and sat down."

"That's it?" Lucien took a step toward the bed.

She indulged herself in a pout. "That's it."

He raised an eyebrow, and his gaze darted to her right ankle and back to her face. "That's quite the sprain."

"I'm clumsy." She bit out the admission. "There's a reason I was on the swim team in high school. I tried running cross-country for one season and my coach literally told my parents he was surprised I ever managed to finish any race on my own two feet."

He was at her bedside, sitting on the edge, still not touching her. "You're really not afraid of me?"

She held his gaze, letting her heart show in her eyes. "You did everything you could to warn me what to expect and everything you said helped me. You're kind of amazing, you know that?"

The corners of his mouth quirked up into a smirk— that smirk she had such a love-hate relationship with. "You think my wolf form is amazing?"

"Not just your wolf form," she muttered. Because if she didn't admit it, he'd probably try to get her to confess later. Better to say so on her own terms.

His smirk deepened.

Taffy chose that moment to hop onto the bed, walk deliberately between them, and lean hard into Ami's hip as he settled himself beside her.

She ruffled the fur between his ears. "You know, I was thinking we still had a mystery."

"Oh?" Lucien's voice was soft, dark. There was that note that sent delicious shivers through her.

"We haven't figured out who set us adrift in the first place." She studied the way Taffy watched Lucien. The corgi's posture was hunched, and she thought Taffy might look a little guilty.

Lucien's back straightened, and the tension in the air shifted to something electric, the way a room sometimes holds a charge when a thunderstorm is gathering. "I didn't scent anyone on the dock. Didn't hear anyone come or go."

She nodded. "You always know who is around you. I haven't been here long, but I've noticed how Trey defers to you. You're aware of everything in the near vicinity in ways I don't even know how to begin describing. If someone snuck up on us at the dock, you would have noticed."

A growl of frustration rolled through the room.

She continued calmly, "I think it was Taffy."

The corgi turned to look at her, his expression distinctly alarmed.

"What?" Lucien's voice was equal parts surprised and incredulous.

She continued her thought process. "He was the only one on the dock and then he wasn't. He was just waiting for us here at the bookstore."

"Was he trying to get rid of us?" Lucien asked sharply.

Taffy growled, then nudged his nose under her hand and whined.

She continued to pet the dog, paying particular attention to the spot he loved at the base of his ears. "I think Taffy realized how close you were to changing. You weren't going to leave me and there wasn't enough time to get you to someplace safe. There was no one else around. So he cast off the ties for the boat and set us adrift. Taffy had faith you wouldn't hurt me. So the safest place for both of us was out on the water."

Taffy looked at her with his soulful brown eyes. He gave her a gentle lick on the inside of her wrist.

Lucien was silent for several minutes. "That'd be hard for a dog to do."

"A normal dog," Ami agreed. "But Taffy is the bookstore's corgi."

The corgi gave her a woof and stood with his deep chest proudly puffed out. She smiled and buried both her hands in his silky fur. Really, he had the softest coat she had ever experienced on a dog. "Good boy, Taffy."

After watching them for another moment, Lucien relented and gave Taffy a firm scratch along his back. "Okay. I believe it. Thanks, fuzzy butt."

Then Lucien caught hold of Ami's hand and threaded his fingers through hers. "So the bookstore corgi saved us and the bookstore itself welcomed you home. You're recognized as the bookstore's Scribe with plenty of town officials willing to witness it, so we just need to take care of the transfer of business ownership. I can have the pack lawyer draw up the paperwork. How do you feel about that?"

"I'd appreciate that." Ami smiled. "To be honest, I came here looking to build a new life for myself, by myself. I've loved the idea of running the bookstore and I've enjoyed rediscovering this small town. I've enjoyed time spent with you."

"But it's been less than a week," Lucien said quietly.

"Yeah." She took a breath and continued. "But I don't feel trapped or boxed in. I don't want to slow down. There's plenty more I want to explore here on the island. There's a lot of questions piling up about you and the supernatural community. I think it'd be scarier if I was trying to process all of that in a bigger place, like Seattle. Wolfsound is enough for me."

And there was Lucien.

"Do you think you'll change your mind in the future?" His question might have been about her staying in Wolfsound or it might have been in reference to more.

"I don't know." Again, it was best to be honest. "But I know what I want right now."

He gave her fingers a gentle squeeze. "What's that?"

"I'd like to explore this thing between us." It was her turn to search his gaze for hints of what he was feeling. The grey of his eyes was stormy. "I don't do one-offs. I'm not interested in friends with benefits."

There was a spark of mischief in his eyes, and his damned smirk was back in full force. "If you take the step to be in a relationship with me—and I am interested in a relationship, to be clear—I don't share."

Ami smiled back, excited fluttering filling her belly and chest. "I'm going to be honest. I have in the past. But that was very specific to the people involved and what we meant to each other, not because I always need relationships to be that way. We are different and I'm happy with it just being between us."

He leaned in until his lips were barely brushing hers. "Did you need more time settling in before getting involved with anyone?"

She pressed her lips against his in answer. His mouth opened to hers as his other hand came up to cup her cheek. They kissed, soft and long, until Taffy sat up and poked a cold nose in between them.

Ami laughed as she leaned back on her pillows. "I think I *am* involved with you, Lucien Allard. All tangled up and completely fallen for you. And I'd really like for you to make love to me right now."

Lucien grinned and kicked Taffy out of the room.

THE END

Thank you for reading *The Ink That Bleeds*. I hope you enjoyed this paranormal cozy mystery!

If you're interested in more paranormal romance elements, give my London Shifters series a try, starting with Bite Me.

Love is hard, especially in the middle of a zombie apocalypse...

I'VE GOT MORE SHIFTER romances and urban fantasy planned soon. Be sure you never miss a new release announcement. Sign up for my newsletter!

WINGS ONCE CURSED & BOUND

COMING APRIL 2023 - ENJOY THIS SNEAK PEEK!

PEERAPHAN

Peeraphan Rahttana closed her eyes and exhaled slowly, letting her senses expand until she was aware of every dancer waiting in the wings, of every stage tech behind the backdrops. It was a part of her warmup when she was on stage, a way for her to get a feel for the people and space around her and prepare for the performance to come. She bent at the hips and reached forward until her fingertips brushed her pointed toes, stretching her muscles as she extended her awareness in a way those around her couldn't —past the empty rows of seats and outward into the halls beyond until she was aware of every stir of air within the theater, of every warm breath taken and given back.

And sensed one presence entering the theatre that... wasn't drawing breath. A person, walking across the front hall who didn't need to breathe.

That couldn't be good.

"Punch! I have the perfect shoes for your performance!" Sirin's strident tone cut into Peeraphan's head more effectively than a physical strike, distracting her momentarily from the unnatural presence she'd sensed.

Of course, Sirin had that effect on Peeraphan—Punch for short—whether the other woman screeched her childhood nickname or not. They'd grown up in the same community and because their parents had been friends, the two of them were supposed to be friendly too, which was why Punch gritted her teeth and smiled.

"Just look at these." Sirin opened a shoe box and shoved the contents forward, practically under Punch's nose. "A very important patron donated these to the production. I think they're antique or something? Either way, they *have* to be in the show."

Punch straightened from her forward stretch and took the box from Sirin's grasp before the other woman managed to actually whack her with it. She opened her mouth to respond, until the most glorious shade of red satin caught her eye and she inadvertently gasped, all irritation with Sirin evaporated, everything else forgotten. The red was luminous, spellbinding even, and she lost the whisper of control she had over her own power as she focused on the shoes.

It wasn't just the heart-stopping color of the shoes. The heels were the perfect height and shape. High and wide enough to accentuate a dancer's legs while still providing stability. They were elegant and sophisticated, tastefully decorated with fine crystal accents and bold enough to be noticed even on stage. They were designed to be a statement.

She needed to put them on. Right away.

Sirin was practically vibrating with excitement. "You have to wear these for the show."

Agreed. No argument there. She needed to put them on. Now.

"No one will be able to say the costumes were lacking when the main dancer has these on her feet," Sirin continued.

No one would be able to take their eyes away from those shoes.

"If they're vintage, they're in amazing condition. You didn't want to wear them?" Punch glanced at Sirin with an effort. Looking away from the shoes for even a moment almost hurt.

But it was odd for Sirin not to want to keep something so clearly special for herself. Throughout their childhood and into adulthood, Sirin did everything it took to be acknowledged as successful. Then she claimed the best of anything she could get her hands on as her reward.

It was a trait Punch kind of hated yet admired about Sirin—the ability to balance doing well and taking credit for her accomplishments.

Punch wasn't just Thai American—, she was a full throwback to something most people in the US wouldn't recognize. Hell, most Thai people, including Sirin, were barely aware of the old folklore.

Because Punch wanted to keep it that way, she had to be careful to hide what she was. It was all well and good to want to stand out from the crowd, shine a little, be unique. But in a lot of ways, that wasn't safe.

Sirin shrugged, crossing her arms over her chest, uncharacteristically chill. "It's obvious they're too small for me and vintage isn't my style. Besides, my shoes were special ordered and dyed to match my costume. You were just going to wear nude-colored character shoes. These are better. You can use today to get used to dancing in them."

The performance was intended to promote awareness of Southeast Asian culture and showcase a fusion of traditional dance and contemporary choreography, with all proceeds going to scholarships for students from marginalized groups. Punch's mother had asked Punch to be a part of the performance as a favor.

"Thai dance, even with a contemporary flare, definitely comes across different with shoes on, especially high-heeled shoes," Punch said, but Sirin was already looking away.

"Let's make sure they fit before we decide they're going with my costume." As amazing as the shoes were, Punch wasn't going to try to wear them if they were a bad fit. Her dance performance could suffer, or worse, she could end up injured. Not worth it, no matter how gorgeous the pair of shoes.

She hoped they fit. She wanted them to fit. Almost *needed* them to fit.

Punch froze, realizing she had already kicked her other shoes off in her eagerness to try them on.

"What are you waiting for, Punch?" Sirin stressed the nickname again, making it sound obnoxious instead of fun.

It had to be on purpose.

The irony was that she liked her own nickname. She'd managed to mostly reclaim it as her own, until she'd agreed to do this performance with Sirin. Seattle was a big city, and yet, here they were, back on a stage together and Punch was yet again wondering how she could shake off the feeling of continually returning to childhood patterns instead of actually making any kind of progress in life.

Do well, but don't show off. Study hard, but never be a know-it-all. Excel, but never brag. Bitterness spread through her mouth as she tasted those memories. All any of it had ever resulted in was a lifetime of unacknowledged accomplishments and second-guessing her own pride in herself. Humility had been drilled into Punch so deeply, daring to take pride in anything felt like a risky dive into arrogance and vanity.

She glanced at the shoes in her hands, so gorgeous. So *red*. She could put on the shoes and this performance could change her life. She felt so sure of it.

There was something wrong. She frowned. Now was not the time to be pondering every personal issue great and small, and her thoughts had been wandering all over the place. She'd sensed something before and hadn't followed up on it.

Other dancers were joining her on the stage, warm-ups complete. Punch reached out with her senses again, scanning the nearly four thousand seat auditorium as she did. There were a few members of the production team sitting in the nearest rows. The air stirred with each exhale and she could feel the minute changes in heat and pressure against her skin the way she imagined fish might sense vibrations in the water around them. There was nothing else, no other living thing in the building. If it moved, even only to breathe, she'd have sensed it. But she'd detected something earlier.

Stage lights caught on crystals decorating the shoes she was holding. Glancing down, Punch admired the glorious red satin. She could see herself dancing inside her mind, wanted to make it real.

The sooner, the better.

She gave in to temptation and bent to slide her left foot into one. The shoe was warm, probably from her own hands, and practically hugged her foot like it'd been molded to fit her specifically. Her left foot was a touch larger than her right by less than half a size—which was why she always tried on the left first—so she might need an extra heel or gel pad. Doable. Better for a shoe to be a touch too big than too small. She put on the other shoe.

Perfect fit. That was weird.

Punch straightened and took a few experimental steps forward. They didn't pinch anywhere and her feet didn't shift or slide around inside the shoes. In fact, the arch support was fantastic.

She couldn't wait to start dancing.

~

BENNETT

Bennett Andrews studied the woman from his vantage point far to the back of the highest mezzanine. She seemed to have been looking out into the audience, searching. Perhaps she had been waiting for someone to come watch the rehearsal. Either way, he had prudently kept to the shadows and waited.

He would have come earlier, if he could have, before the red shoes had claimed a victim.

His consortium had received a tip the other day about the red shoes surfacing at Pike Place Market. Truly, one could find just about anything there, particularly if one knew where to shop in the deeper levels of the market. He'd tracked the seller down but had encountered complications following up with the buyer until he'd been forced to retire with the sunrise. The consortium's witch had managed to detect the presence of the red shoes in the meantime, pinpointing their location within this theater. He'd come as soon as he'd risen for the evening, sooner than any other of his brethren in the region could have.

It hadn't been quick enough.

He was not here to catch attention, and it would be best if the woman did not remember seeing anyone out of the ordinary—assuming she survived—so he hadn't used his enhanced abilities to reach her, instead moving into the theater at a normal *human* pace. As she joined the other dancers in formation and music began playing, he thought the chances of her living beyond the evening were low. Miniscule.

She had already put on the red shoes, after all.

At this point, there was nothing for it but to wait for the screams and chaos and panic, then choose a moment in all the confusion to remove the shoes from the corpse. Even if he'd failed to come in time to prevent the death of this victim, he could do his best to ensure there wouldn't be another.

The music started and the dancer with the red shoes was quite good, actually. Based on his research, the shoes compelled the wearer to dance, but they did not augment their skill. This woman was talented, with a compelling presence that drew the eye wherever she was on stage, whether she was the principle or dancing in a supporting role. She was incredibly expressive, every line of her body projecting her interpretation of the music, and she was light on her feet, making challenging leaps and turns look easy.

She was so full of life, he scowled. It would take that much more time for the shoes to drive her past exhaustion and beyond collapse. Thomas would call him an asshole for thinking that way, but the longer it took, the worse it would be for her. He hoped, for her sake as well as his own, that this was quick.

The red shoes were particularly cruel, according to some versions of the fairy tale, with roots in the Nordic lands of Northern Europe. If allowed to pass from hand to hand, human to human, there would be a trail of deaths left in their wake. Better for him to stop them here, after this one last death, and take them so the fairy tale could fade back into nothing but a barely remembered story.

"Okay! Let's break for five!" The director clapped her hands.

The chaos would start soon, once the dancer with the red shoes realized she had no choice but to keep on dancing. The shoes would compel her to increase intensity and speed until she literally worked herself into oblivion.

There had been a time when he would have allowed himself more sympathy for the doomed human. He'd learned since then that the pain of such feelings weren't within his capacity to endure. One could only witness death so many times without developing coping mechanisms to endure. He pulled his hands out of his coat pockets and prepared to move as soon as everyone was distracted.

But the dancer not only stopped, she walked over to what were presumably her belongings and sat down, reaching for a water bottle.

Surprise rippled through him, the unfamiliar sensation like a static shock. She wasn't even tapping her toes.

He frowned. Something wasn't right. There must be some mistake. Those shoes might not be the ones he was here for.

He would have to get closer to be sure.

Traveling the distance from the upper balcony, past the carefully preserved artwork and furniture of the lobbies of three different floors, to find his way backstage took seconds. He could move at speeds that were a blur to the human eye, and as the evening was deepening to full dark, his abilities woke even further. In full night, few things in the world were safe from him. His talents had evolved to make him one of the most efficient hunters on Earth, among a host of beings whose existence humankind had forgotten. Humans were not the apex predators of the world.

As he found himself an out of the way spot where he could look across the stage from the wings, he realized with another jolt that the woman wearing the red shoes was *aware* of him. Even more interesting, she was not staring. Her gaze was cast downward as she sipped her bottle of water and she was sneaking furtive glances his way under the cover of lowered lashes. Based on her body posture, she was not frightened, or at least not panicked. Her back was straight, shoulders relaxed. Her feet were drawn close under her but spread enough for her to launch in whatever direction might be necessary. He imagined she was on alert and ready to bolt, but she was, he thought, giving him the most epic side eye he had ever had cast in his direction.

And vampires at their most arrogant made disapproval and scorn an art form.

He smiled; he couldn't help himself.

Unable to resist, he began noting details about her. She was petite, compared to him and most of the company he had been keeping lately. But then, they were mostly men of six feet in height or more. Even the women and nonbinary among his organization were closer to six feet in height. Among the other dancers, though, she was one of the larger built, with a robust frame and more generous curves. It wasn't just tits and ass, as the old Broadway musical put to song, but the curve of well-defined muscle over her shoulders and upper arms, over her thighs and calves. She reminded him more of a warrior, capable of delivering heavy strikes and devastating blows balanced by flexibility, agility, and grace. With training, he imagined her capable of quite the killing dance on a battlefield. But those times were long gone, by human standards. Humans had invented ways to wage war from a distance with massively destructive results.

She was dressed in comfortable athletic wear with her dark brown hair twisted up into a bun, and her feet trapped in a pair of brilliant red shoes which were definitely the pair he had come to acquire. They reeked of cursed magic, a blend of seductive suggestion and poisonous animosity. They'd been imbued centuries ago with a single intent: redemption of sins or the death of the wearer.

He had not taken more than a glance at her face. In fact, he refused to learn to recognize her, if at all possible. He had only met her across a distance, and he was already sure the memory of her dancing would haunt his nightmares despite every effort he'd made to keep up an icy wall of indifference once she died. And he had an eternity to wrestle with remembrance. He had learned the hard way it was wiser to maintain as much emotional distance as possible from the mortals he met.

So no, thank you, he did not plan to add her face to the other poor victims he had gotten to know before he had failed to save them.

But now he was confronted with an issue. The mythic items he had come to acquire were indeed here. He needed to take them into custody before someone else with greater malicious intent did. He couldn't just walk up and take them off her feet without her attracting too much attention. She wasn't likely to believe him if he told her the shoes were trying to kill her either. She was resisting them, somehow. Which also meant he could not assume she was doomed. It might simply be a matter of time, a quirk. Or it might be a chance for her—one in who knew how many—to survive.

"Break's over!" One of the other humans—the director —clapped her hands together. "Let's run the number from the top."

The woman in the red shoes shot him another glance, then put her water bottle aside and began to stand. She was going to dance again and this time, she might not be able to stop. This was not as simple as acquiring the shoes anymore. He was in a position to prevent a tragedy.

If he cared about her life.

It was one thing to commit himself to a cause for the better of the world, but it was completely different when it came to saving a specific life. It required too much...humanity. And that was something he had been working to leave behind for too long.

She was on her feet, stepping toward the stage.

"Don't." The word was out of his mouth before he could stop himself.

You can pre-order Wings Once Cursed & Bound now!

~

My wings unbound, I am the Thai bird princess
—I am the kinnaree—
And no matter the cost,
I will be free.

Peeraphan Rahttana lives her life in Seattle, unaware of the complicated magical world spinning just beyond the shadows and mist...until a violent clash outside her dance rehearsal has her *literally* whisked off her feet. Her darkly brooding rescuer, vampire Bennet Andrews, claims to represent a secret organization dedicated to locating objects of myth and magic, tucking them safely away where they can do no harm—but he's too late to save Peeraphan from a deadly curse.

Yet Peeraphan isn't what she seems. Wings unbound, she's a Thai bird princess of legend...and while the curse won't kill her outright, it's only a matter of time. Determined, Bennett sweeps Peeraphan deeper into a supernatural world far beyond anything she ever imagined in a desperate bid to find a solution...and an explanation for the powers even she doesn't know how to define.

Her world may have changed overnight, but Peeraphan knows one thing for certain: she can't go back to living as a human anymore. Not when she's felt what it's like to fly with Bennet by her side. She's determined to keep her wings and her freedom...and defy anyone who would try to take them from her again.

ACKNOWLEDGMENTS

Thank you to Matthew. Without you I might never have written this story or created this series. Your encouragement and enthusiasm for this story was invaluable.

Thank you to Tara Rayers, my editor. This story truly tightened up and improved with your feedback.

Thank you to Katee Robert and Asa Maria Bradley for anchoring me as I flailed wildly in my excitement over this idea, and to Gail Carriger for your wit and brilliant feedback.

Finally, thank you to my readers. You make sharing my stories a joy and I hope you love the characters in this one as much as I do.

ABOUT THE AUTHOR

Piper J. Drake is a bestselling author of romantic suspense, paranormal romance, science fiction, and fantasy.

Gamer. Foodie. Wanderer. Usually not lost.

Piper aspires to give her readers stories with a taste of the hard challenges in life, a breath of laughter, a broad range of strengths and weaknesses, the sweet taste of kisses, and the heat of excitement across multiple genres.

Want the earliest updates, sneak peeks, and exclusive content from Piper? Sign up for her newsletter.